THE ONLY MATE

MILLIE LAWSON

Contents

CHAPTER ONE

The Staring

Ella POV

I walked into my new school. I could feel the nervous chills running down my spine. I had just moved from Tennessee with my uncle Dan. In his opinion, it was time for a new scene which meant someone started noticing my bruises, and bruises meant trouble. I'm not too fond of new schools. Everyone always stares at you and asks you questions like where you from?

I've always been a bit shy, I guess. I'm not fond of meeting new people. It's always sounded like a risk. In some ways, it's a blessing the more secluded I am, the longer we stay.

As I opened the door to the entrance of my new, he'll hole. I was instantly greeted with stares from my new fellow schoolmates. I knew why they were staring; not only am I new, but I'm also very short; I stand a little over 5'4, but I round it up to five.

It's probably because of my uncle. I've never been given the proper meals or diet. I stopped growing in sixth grade. When all the girls got their growth spurts, I was left behind like always.

I decided not to wear my platform vans which at about an inch, instead I went for a pair of black High-top converse I found at the thrift store in our last town. I wore a long sleeve dress with black tights to hide any evidence of my uncle.

As I walked down towards the door with the signing office above it, I entered to find the receptionist. She was old and by old, I mean prune wrinkled old. She looked up as I entered with her thick-framed glasses.

"Hello dear, how can I help you?" She asked with a sweet grand-ma-like tone.

"Hello Ma'am, my name is Ella Lynn. I'm new to this school and was told to get my schedule here" She smiled up at me and handed me several papers, one with my schedule and one with a map of Green Everest High.

"You just have the sweetest accent, dear; where did you move from," she said

"Oh, well, I was born in Virginia but was raised in Tennessee. We move around quite a bit." I plastered a smile on my face.

"Okay dear, well, I hope you have a great first day. "And with that, I left the office.

As I looked at my schedule, I wasn't surprised by all my regular classes. I was ahead in school and took college-level classes even though I'm a junior. At Green Everest High, you have to take two electives. I was assigned art and home etc. So my first class was calculus.

I loved math. Crazy right? I don't know what it was about it, but I just liked knowing that there was always a solid answer, no mistakes. Looking at the map, I saw that my class was down the hall and to the left. As I walked, I felt eyes staring at me, not like how the other kids looked at me but staring looking around over my shoulder I saw him.

He had dark brown hair short on the sides but a little long on the top. His green eyes were so bright I could see the color even when he stood about 6 meters away from me. He was tall, very, very tall, like 6'5, no joke! I looked like a midget compared to him. He had a strong jaw and a little bit of stubble on his chin. His lips were just the right size and looked so kissable. He was muscular but in a friendly way, not a scary way. He was beautiful.

Omg, I'm staring. Stop staring!! I turned around quickly and walked straight into my class.

Hey you guys, I just wanted to say I never thought this book would get any readers. I

CHAPTER TWO

Shortie

L evi

I couldn't stop staring at her; she was beautiful. She had to be less than five feet tall, but she was breathtaking. She had long brown hair which landed in loose curls down to her hips. She was skinny, maybe a little too thin. I wanted to take her home to the pack and cook for her.

I thought it couldn't get better, but then she turned her head around and looked me straight in the eyes. Her eyes were a gorgeous ocean blue. As I trailed down her face, I took in her delicate features. She had these rosy cheeks spotted with freckles that cover the bridge of her cute little button nose. Then there were her lips that were plump and pink, so delicious. I just wanted to kiss her.

What? Why? She's human. I could smell it even though she smelt amazing. She smelt like strawberries right when they're ripe. I have to stop staring.

"Remember we have a mate!" My inner wolf growled.

"I know Cody, I remember, but boy do I want her to be it!"

My wolf scowled at me for ignoring his warning. I wasn't going to ask her out or anything; I'm just going to observe her. He's right, and I know it. I, too, wouldn't be happy if our true mate was checking out someone other than us. It's a territorial thing.

I couldn't help but deflate when her eyes left mine, turned back around, and quickly walked away. But then the unthinkable happened, and Shortie walked into my calculus class. I rushed into the room to see her talking to Mr. Burns, our teacher. He pointed to the empty seat in the back right in front of mine. Yes, I get to smell strawberries all period. I grinned at this, although once again, my wolf wasn't too happy.

As I sat down and looked to the side, I saw my future beta. He sat in the seat next to me. Carter is my right-hand man. I loved him like he was my brother. Carter and I looked a little similar. I mean, we are cousins, but he was a little shorter than I and less buff, but his wolf was just as large as mine. Too bad he wasn't as strong. Carter has been my best friend since birth practically. We have baby pictures of us strewn all over my house walls.

"Hey Bro, how's your morning? Didn't see you when I left the house? When did you even get up?" Carter questioned.

" Left early, woke up around 6:00. I had to go see Mrs. Shirley about my essay," I stated bluntly.

I had done an excellent job on the essay but apparently, too good of a job now my teacher now wants me to join her college English class. With all my Alpha training and pack business, It's going to be a lot more work on my hands, but of course, Mrs. Shirley didn't take no for an answer.

"Hey, who's she" he whispered, elbowing my shoulder and proceeding to start pointing at Shortie.

" I don't know," yet I mumbled.

Right as the class settled in, our teacher Mr. Burns introduced Shortie to everyone.

"As you can see, class, we have a new student amongst us. Could you introduce yourself and tell us three things about yourself."

The brown-haired beauty rose from her seat and looked around at everyone before answering.

"Hello, y'all; my name is Ella Lynn, but everyone calls me Ellie. I just moved from Tennessee. I'm 16 years old, and I also love dogs."

She has an accent, damn, and she'd be the perfect mate!

CHAPTER THREE

His Name

Ella POV

I am stuck in class learning about formulas I'm supposed to use to solve all the equations on our worksheet. Calculus with Mr. Burns was boring as hell. While Mr. Burns was in the middle of talking, I felt a pencil stab me in the back. I turned around in my seat, looking straight into forest green eyes. The brown-haired boy shook his head with a smile on his face and pointed the kid next to him. The boy looked just like him, except his hair was a lighter brown, and his skin was paler, and he wasn't as attractive.

"Hi, my name is Carter. Aren't you a little too young to be in a college course class?" He smirked in a fake accent.

I hated being judged and or mocked in any way. I turned to him and looked him dead in the eyes.

"Aren't you a little too dumb to be in a college course class," I said in my sweet country accent? Burn.

Carter's smirk turned into a full-blown smile. I turned my head and looked at the brown-haired boy. He had an amused smile placed on his pretty face. God, was he ever so handsome.

"May I ask you what your name is?"

"Levi."

"Well, you already know my name." I giggled and turned around to listen to what our teacher was saying.

Class ended faster than I thought. I went through all my morning classes in a breeze, and I also succeeded in keeping to myself. Thankfully none of my other teachers had me introduce myself, which made my life much easier. The cafeteria was busy, and people were everywhere. The school had an indoor cafeteria filled with tables, and then there was the schoolyard which was a bunch of grass outside the cafeteria where you could sit if you pleased.

The cafeteria was filled, and students were either gossiping or wrestling with one another. Not my cup of tea.

The yard had several trees including a Jacaranda tree. Barely anyone was in the yard, so being my antisocial self, I plopped myself down in front of the tree and let my backrest on the smooth trunk. It was nice outside today. It wasn't too hot or too cold; it was perfect.

I went through my backpack in search of my Chromebook. The school provided everyone with their laptop to do homework on. I opened it up, logging in, and opened a new tab. As I tap the search key, I typed in available jobs in the Evercrest area. Only six positions came up, and I was only qualified for one, a waitress at the local diner in town. Seizing the opportunity, I emailed them my application and resume and prayed they would email me back.

Once I had finished, the bell had rung. My next class was home EC. Home EC was an okay class. All we did was learn about how to do our future taxes. Which I already knew because my uncle refuses to do them. My last class of the day was college English. I walked into the class finding the classroom filled with couches, beanbags, and armchairs. There was even an ottoman. My new teacher's name was Mrs. Shirley.

She was short like me with wild red hair. She made me think of the teacher from the magic school bus. After entering, I sat down on one of the empty armchair's waiting for our class to begin. Right as everyone settled in, Levi entered the class. I couldn't take my eyes off him. Oh my gosh, was I drooling good? Could I be any more pathetic? Before I looked away, he saw me and just smirked. Ughhh, could he be any more infuriating?

CHAPTER FOUR

Uncle

EllaEnglish class ended, and it was my overall favorite class, and my least favorite was art. I lack in the creativity category. I left the class along with the rest of my classmates and started walking home. The house Dan and I live in are about a 30-minute walk from the school. I don't mind walking through it's soothing hearing my feet tap against the pavement while I walk to my little beat. It's around 3:40 when I arrive home.

The house is blue but needs a paint job. Most of the tiles in the home are cracked, and parts of the carpet are stained. It's my favorite place I've lived with Dan so far. Why? Well, all the doors have locks on them. The last few houses we lived in didn't have a lock on the bathroom door. I would always take a chair in the bathroom with me to put up against the door. I did the same thing to my bedroom door. It was my only extra protection from Dan and his slimy friends.

Several of the houses we lived at did little to keep me comfortable and safe. So from a young age, you pick up things. Always find a way to lock the door. Don't get too close to a stove you've never used in an old house, and always make sure you have an exit route. As I walked into the house, I quickly head down the hallway and enter my room, quietly shutting the door. If Dan is asleep, I don't want to be the one to wake him up. That would cause problems. Once the door is shut, I run to my bed and pull my laptop out of my backpack. As I go to my email, I see what I've been waiting for an email from the diner's manager asking for an interview. The manager Hank wants me to be interviewed tomorrow at 4:30. Perfect!!! I respond to the email, agreeing to meet him at the diner.

I am putting the laptop away and sticking it in my backpack. Knowing that I've had a long day, I put on my pajamas. I've had the same pair of Hello Kitty pajamas since 5th grade. They've started to thin out, and soon after I get a job, I'll be able to buy some new ones finally.

I walk into the bathroom quickly and shut the door softly to avoid any noise, and start brushing my teeth. I was blessed with my mother's straight teeth and small nose; my dad gave me his thick hair. I look at my body dissatisfaction echoed on my face. I hate how thin and short I am. We don't know where I get my height from. I looked week and pale. I started weaving my hair into a French braid down my back. To keep it out of my face and to prevent tangles as I sleep. That way, all I have to do in the morning is unbraid and let the waves loose. After washing my face, I headed off to bed. I was hungry, but Dan hasn't gone to the store yet, and if I bothered him, I'd get a beating.

I slowly entered my room, making sure to lock the door and tucked myself in, praying that someday my life would be different, that I'd be different, that I'd have someone to embrace me in love and affection, and I return to give him my everything.

Closing my eyes, I dreamt of a beautiful life with the brown-haired boy.

CHAPTER FIVE

Mine

Levi POV

"Happy Birthday!" Screamed my parents and Carter.

"It's 6 am. What the hell". I grumbled and rolled back to and try and sleep. School is in two hours. I don't know what they're thinking birthday or not. I need my sleep.

I'm not a morning person, but who even is besides my parents? Ughh, I can't go back to sleep guess I'll get up.

Since I'm eighteen, I will officially be the Alpha of the Moon Ridge pack. All I need now is my mate, which hopefully I'll find today now that I'm old enough to find her.

I walk into my restroom and look in the mirror. I have serious bed head. I go through my usual routine. I chose to wear a navy blue T-shirt with my jeans.

Mmmm, mom made waffles. I walk down to the kitchen, and there is a steaming plate of waffles.

"Alpha," Carter smirks. I swear that guy's ass, but for some reason, I can't get rid of him. My dad turns to give him a dirty look. You never want to disrespect the Alpha or the elders.

"So, son, are you excited to get out there and meet your mate? Remember, if you don't find her in our pack, you can always travel to the others."

My mother was from another pack. The Crimson Keepers their well-known; their Alpha is a great leader and very helpful to our pack. I don't believe my mates in another pack.

My wolf is getting agitated.

"What do you want, Cody?"

"We need to leave she's out their"

I have to leave. I can feel the need if I don't go. He will come out and scare the shit out of people. Here I go.

CHAPTER SIX

Perfect

Warning this chapter contains abuse and starvation this may be triggering.Ella POV

Bang! Bang!

What the hell! I woke up to Dan trying to break into my room. It's three in the morning!

"Hey slut open up!"

I ignore him. He's probably drunk and high, and when he's like that, I don't know what will happen.

Last month Dan got a little handsy, and when I pulled away from him, he punched me in the eye and continued to beat me. Bruises covered my entire stomach in bruises. Luckily I didn't get a broken rib from the blows.

"Hey, come on, open the door, let's have some fun."

Ya, how about not. I tried to go back to sleep when the door broke open. Dan was a big guy. He had muscle which scares me.

He started to stalk over to me. His eyes rolled over my body. My nightgown left nothing to the imagination; it was thin. I pulled my blanket up to hide any part of myself from him.

"Oh, you don't need to hide anything from me." He chuckled out.

At that moment, I realized if I didn't leave now, I'd be raped. I looked around my room. Next to my bed was the lamp; it was just big enough to cause minor damage. I couldn't let him get to me.

"Ella, you have always had a nice body" his lingering eyes land on my face, and he smirks. He started walking to the side of my bed. I could smell him; he reeked of body odor and booze.

I was pretty fast for being so small. Dan started getting closer to me. It was now or never. I grabbed the lamp from the table, stood up on my bed, and hit him as hard as I could. He fell over in a massive heap on the floor. I looked around my room. I needed to get dressed; it was too early to head to school, but I had no choice. I grabbed my backpack, put in a change of clothes, and ran to the bathroom to change. I had to be quick; he could wake up any minute.

I pulled on my jeans and my long sleeve navy shirt. It was simple and easy to undo my braids, racking my fingers hastily through the waves. I go to Dan's room. He usually kept cash in his bedside drawer along with a box of condoms. I discovered this last year when we needed groceries. I searched his room for money.

Grabbing the stack of hundreds, I put them in my back pocket. I run out of the house and head to the school.

I want to cry. I haven't called since my parents. I need to get out of here get away from him. He won't look for me even if I did steal that money; he wouldn't care.

I was alone, and I'm okay with that. My life isn't perfect, but maybe things will get better.

The schools still empty as the hour's pass. I sat on the ground under the beautiful branches of the jacaranda tree, thinking. I was getting out. I got the job interview today, and nothing was stopping me from getting the job. I knew there was a motel about three miles away from the school.

Around 5:30, the school opens. I walk into the cafeteria and get their complimentary breakfast. It was cereal today and an apple. I was so grateful for the food. I hadn't eaten for a while and needed the energy. Just as I'm finishing up, a small girl comes and sits in front of me. As I look up at her, she smiles.

"Hi, I'm Avery," she squeaks out.

"Hi, I'm Ellie; it's nice to meet you," I say back.

Her face instantly turns into a beautiful smile. She was pretty. Avery had olive skin and golden-brown eyes. Her hair was dark brown and very smooth. Avery wolfed her cereal; she was skinny like me. To the point where you look somewhat starved. Her clothes were too baggy on her like me. I knew wherever Avery was from wasn't much better than where I was.

We made a small chat and talked about our classes and the teachers. Grace didn't start for another hour, so we decided to walk to the library. We quietly did our homework at a table in the back. I liked being around Avery. She wasn't loud, and silence wasn't awkward.

We went our separate ways and planned to meet at lunch under the Jacaranda tree.

Walking down the hall, I smelled something unique. It was a mixture of cinnamon and spice; it was terrific. I looked around to see where it was coming from. That's when I saw Levi. Was it him? Not possible he was too far away. When our eyes locked before I could blink, He was standing in front of me within seconds. His face had a brilliant smile plastered on it. He was so beautiful.

"Mate," he whispered.

"What?" I mumbled. I could barely speak. I was so entranced by him his smell overwhelmed my senses. His hand slowly reached up and fell on my cheek. His touch was soft and sent tingles all over. My body felt as if it was electrified. One word left my lips in that second.

"You're mine."

Chapter Seven

Growling

Hey readers I just wanted to say thank you for reading my book so far!!! I hope you guys like it and continue to read please vote or leave a comment. xoxo-Lillian

Levi POV

"You're mine," she whispered

My wolf howled in pride. She wants me. I look into her blue eyes; she's so beautiful. She had her long hair down. It was full of waves; she looked gorgeous.

I was going to marry this woman. We are going to mate and have our pups together and grow old together. I could see it all. She was young, but I can wait. I'd wait forever just for her.

All of a sudden, her eyes got wide as she let out a gasp.

"Oh my god! I'm so sorry. I don't know what just came over me? Did you need help with something?"

My chest deflated at her words, and my pride was pretty much thrown out the window. She doesn't know what I am; she must think I'm a creep walking up to her.

"Mark her; then she will love us!"

Do you realize how dumb you are? We can mark her in the middle of the hallway!

I want mate! Cody growled.

I needed to come up with something to say. I need her near me. What if I scare her and she doesn't want me?

"I uh wanted to ask you out? Uh, yea, ask you out" oh boy, was I in trouble. I must look like a complete goon.

Ella

He was so cute he looked completely flustered with what he was saying. I couldn't believe he was asking me out. I wanted to reach up and grab his blushing face and kiss him. Too bad I'm too short.

Looking him in the eyes, I decided. For once in my life, I knew Dan wasn't going to be there watching over me. I was free to make friends and fall in love. I could love Levi, and maybe I somewhat already did.

Looking up, I smiled and said what I've always wanted to say.

"Yes"

"You want to go? Yes!" Levi's smile was enchanting. He started to blush even more, which in return made me also blush. An undeniable urge to hug him cane over by, and I took a step forward and hugged him. His strong arms wrapped around me my entire body shivered in pleasure. I felt secure, and yet he held me in his arms so gently as if

I was the most fragile piece of glass. I've never been held like this or not that I've remembered. I knew I made the right decision.

I didn't want to leave his grasp. I just yearned to be in his arms. He didn't let go of me even when I pulled away from him; he kept his hands on my hips. His eyes shined with something I couldn't yet identify; it was of want and need, but something else lingered there, and for some reason, it drew me to him even more.

He walked us to class, where we sat in our seats with him behind me. Carter has entered the classroom a little while afterward. He smiled at me and gave me a signature player wink. At that moment, I heard Levi growl. Like an actual growl.

Carter's face became ashen, and his eyes widened as they turned to me. I turned in my seat to get a better view of Levi; he and carter were weirdly looking at each other. It was as if they were talking to scooter without saying a word; it was freaking weird. With that, I turned away and faced the front, waiting for the class to start.

CHAPTER EIGHT

Whipped

Levi POV

Mr. Burns was going on about god knows what during his lecture, but all I was focused on was Ella. She smelled terrific; her strawberry scent was intoxicating. My wolf was finally content.

Although I was happy, I was also annoyed. Carter kept trying to mind link to me, but I was ignoring his ass. I could tell he was pissed at me for blocking him; he was fidgeting in his chair.

Ella was writing notes. I peeked over her shoulder to see what she was writing, and in perfect cursive, she was taking her notes. She was so unique and wonderful; all her I's had hearts. Damn, was that cute.

She turns her head, and her eyes came to look into mine; her eyes were so blue I got lost in them. They wear eyes I could look into forever and never complain; then they got very wide in shock as she looked away from me. Why did she turn away? Coming back to earth, I saw Mr. Burns frowning towards me.

He was looking at me, waiting for a response to a question I didn't hear. Looking over to Carter, I unblocked him so he could tell me the question.

"What's the answer for the variable b?"

Looking at the board, I answer the question immediately.

" B is equal to thirteen to the sixth power."

Mr. Burns turned to the board and back to me, nodded in approval, and then finished his lesson. I'm good at school. I should've graduated a while ago, but I wanted to stay with my friends. It's not like I was going to college or anything once I graduate. I take on the complete and full responsibility of Alpha.

I was ready for it, but I still need a Diploma. The bell was supposed to ring in two minutes, packing up my backpack. I got up and stood in front of Ella. Her beautiful eyes once again got large as I somewhat startled her. She grabbed her bag and slowly rose from her desk. As she tried to squeeze past me, I took it as my opportunity to hold her hand. Jolts of pure bliss entered my body through her touch. Her small hands fit perfectly in my large ones.

"Why-y are y-you holding my hand?" She breathed out.

"Because I want to" I smiled down at her.

Her cheeks turned a bright shade of pink. Boy, oh boy, I was whipped; this little lady had me tied around her finger, and I was happy to be there.

Ella

His hand was so warm and large I loved how it engulfed mine perfectly. His hands were soft. The tingles I got from holding onto him were brilliant. Walking out of class, people started to stare at us. So girls glared, and while some smiled at me, encouraging me. I was on cloud nine. Just being with him made me so happy.

I looked up at his handsome face to see him looking back at me with his green eyes. He walked me to my science class, and when I was about to walk away to enter the classroom, he tightened his hold on my hand and pulled me towards him. I land straight into his chest; my entire body lit up with joy. He made me feel so amazing. Looking up to him, he smiled down at me and wrapped his hands around my waist. Leaning down gently, he placed a kiss on my cheek. It was so gentle and sweet it made my face turn as red as a tomato. Turning away, I whispered bye and walked into chemistry.

My morning classes went by pretty quickly. The entire morning my head was spinning. All I could think about was Levi.

I walked toward the jacaranda tree to see Avery standing underneath it, smiling up at me. We waved at each other, and after we set our book bags down, we headed towards the cafeteria. We both got free lunch today was outlets lucky day it was a spicy chicken sandwich, with milk, carrots, and a fruit of choice. I chose another apple finding them more appealing than an orange. Our sandwiches consisted of a large chicken nugget in between hamburger buns.

Although our food may have seemed unappealing, I was lucky today's lunch would keep me full till tomorrow morning. We headed back to the tree and sat down, and finished our food silently.

" what are you doing after school today?" Avery asked as she turned towards me. She had a carrot halfway up to her mouth, waiting for a reply.

" I have a job interview. I'm so excited," I said, smiling back at her.

We continued to talk about everything and nothing. I was so caught up in our conversation I hadn't noticed Levi until he sat down right beside me.

" Hey, what are you doing outside? Nobody's out there?" He asked, concern lacing his voice. I don't understand why he was so worried about me being alone. It was just Avery and me, so technically, we weren't alone. We had each other. I enjoyed being alone; it gave me time to think for myself.

"Avery's with me" I smiled at him, turning to Avery. She waved shyly and immediately looked down.

" Come have lunch with me. It'll be fun; my friends are dying to meet you?" Levi was so cute she was smiling down at me, all excited. I hated to burst his bubble, but I wasn't fond of crowds and meeting new people.

I liked being around Avery; she was sweet, and she was like me; we both weren't in the best situations. I could instantly trust her because we were sadly two of the same.

I turned over to look at Levi and whispered my answer, " No, thank you, I'm fine right here; Avery and I are having fun" I smile at Avery as she smiles back at my response. I had chosen her over a group of kids, and I knew it meant a lot to her.

Levi's face fell into a frown, and as if a light had switched back on, he smiled back at me.

" Then I guess I'll just have to eat here with you." He winked.

CHAPTER NINE

Charlie's

Levi POV

I felt a tinge of pain for her not wanting to eat lunch with my friends and me. They were all from the pack, and soon she would be there, Luna. She would play a huge role in my decisions as a mate and a wife.

Ella looked a bit uncomfortable because of my offer, so when she said no, I knew I'd have to stay with her. I needed to plan the date I hadn't exactly planned on. Maybe she likes movies? Or a nice dinner? I'm not exactly sure if it were up to me, we would go down to Charlie's Diner. It's the only burger place in town we don't even have a McDonald's. Everest is a tiny town population is about 20,000, about a tenth of which is the pack.

Looking down at my beautiful angel, I'm even more anxious to go on our date, so we're all alone.

"Ellie, what are you doing after school today?" I ask

"Oh, I just asked Ella the same question," Avery giggles.

" I'm going to a job interview today," Ella smiles as she replies.

I don't want my girl working. I'll support her; of course, I'm not against her working, but she's just so skinny. I want her to eat more, and then she can. I don't know why she is so underweight. Does she eat at home?

I look at Ellie at smile down at her. Only if she knew how much I want to care for her.

"Where is the interview?"

"Well, I do believe it's at y'all's diner in town, Charlie's," she says with her sweet voice.

Damn, she's working at Charlie's. Not only is it my favorite place to eat, but the owner, Charlie, is part of my pack. It's not very common for a pack member to live and work outside of our boundaries, but we've made an exception for Charlie. He's a good man, and I know him and his mate Lucy will take good care of my girl.

"That's great. I'm sure you will get the position."

On that note, I better talk to Charlie to make sure she gets the position.

'Charlie'

'Yes, Alpha?'

'Hire Ella and treat her well. She is your future, Luna.'

'Yes, Alpha!'

Now that that's settled, I can stare at my beautiful mate until the bell rings.

Ella POV

Levi does this weird staring thingy, and it's starting to creep me out. He will stare at nothing for a solid minute and then stare at me for another twenty. What's so interesting do I have food on my face? Is there a bug in my hair? I've finally had enough.

"What are you staring at?" I question, giving him the stink eye.

His face lightens up, and he smiles at me even more and gives me the most intelligent answer any man could give a woman.

" pure beauty"

Yes, my heart just stopped in my chest, and my cheeks turned as red as a tomato. Avery started giggling, and Carter gave us both a disgusted face.

Damn.

CHAPTER TEN

Romeo

Ella POV

School went by pretty fast. Before I knew it, I was sitting down in Mrs. Shirley's class.

This was by far my favorite class. Mrs. Shirley's class is full of books. She has all the classics, but she also has some new ones.

We had just started reading Romeo and Juliet. I had already read it at one of my old schools. It's recommended for sophomores, but Evercrest didn't have reading requirements. It was all up to the teachers.

"Okay, class, who wants to volunteer to be the voice of Juliet?"

I hated that she had the class voice the scenes. She turned her head and looked around the room for her future victims.

"No one wants to volunteer? Okay, I guess it's my lucky day. Ellie, why don't you be our Juliet." She stated, smiling brightly at me.

She started looking for a partner to be Romeo. Her eyes landed on Carter.

"Cart-"

"I have to be Romeo!" Yelled Levi. Scaring our entire class, including me.

Levi's face was so cute he started to blush after he outroars. Carter had a smirk smeared on his face as he stared at Levi.

"Okay, then Levi is our Romeo, Carter; you can be Tybalt."

After she finished naming off who plays who, we begin our reading.

"That which we call a rose

By any other name would smell as sweet; So Romeo would were he not Romeo call'd, Retain that dear perfection which he owes.

Without that title. Romeo, doff thy name, And for that name, which is no part of thee, Take all myself." I read

It was Levi's turn to read, but he just sat there staring at me with pure happiness in his eyes. He sat there with his dopey smile until Mrs. Shirley told him to read.

Levi

I loved listening to her read. Her voice is so sweet, and I could smell her from where I was sitting. Only if she could read to me all day long, I could never be bored.

"Levi?" Mrs. Shirley hissed. That's my queue.

"I take thee at thy word. Call me but love, and I'll be new baptis'd; Henceforth, I never will be Romeo." I said as I watched my beauty blush.

She always blushed; her cute little face got all rosy, somewhat hiding her freckles.

We continued our reading until the bell rang, and with that, I got up and walked toward my love.

"Hello, there, sweetheart." I smile down; damn, she was so short, but for such a shortie, she was beautiful.

"Hello," she whispered, her cheeks getting even redder.

"What are you doing right now?"I asked

"Walking to the bus," she bluntly stated.

Oh yeah, she has that interview thingy today; the diner is about a thirty-minute walk from school but a twelve-minute bus ride.

" Can I drive you there? I mean to the diner?" My face felt as if it was on fire at this very moment.

Her eyes lit up, and she nodded her head slightly, and with that, I took her dainty little hand in mine as we left the classroom.

We walked through the halls and out the door to the parking lot. I drove a dark shiny blue 2020 mustang. It may seem like much, but it's my baby. I partially own a multi-billion dollar company with my father as the alpha you have to make money to support your own.

Ella stops looking back at her; I can see her eyes bugging out. I tug on her arm lightly, and she comes back into reality and walks up to our car.

Ella

He drives a sports car. He drives a sports car. No big deal, it's no big deal. Levi unlocks the doors, and I open them to reveal a smooth black leather interior. The car smells new and is extremely clean.

Sitting down, I'm engulfed in the smell of both new leather and Levi himself. I feel so at peace. Levi hops in and turns the key in the ignition. The car roars to life. We speed out of the school's parking lot and onto the street; the car purrs as we drive down the road towards the diner. We get there in five minutes. Levi pulls into a parking space with perfect precision.

I don't need to be inside for the next thirty minutes. The interview was supposed to be at 4:30, and here we are at 3:00.

Looking over to Levi, I see his eyes studying me; his lips curve up into his million-dollar smile as he finds he's been caught looking at me. He takings my hand into his lap and gives it a gentle squeeze as he brings it up to his lips and kisses the back of it softly. His eyes are full of so much love and care all I want to do is crawl over the console and into his lap.

Looking into my eyes, he whispers to me. "Hey, Babe, are you ready? Let's go get a shake before you start, okay?" His voice was so sweet as if charming without any hesitation; I smile and nod.

Charlie's diners small and cute it has a 1950s kind of look to it with a black and white checkered floor and restored red leather booths. All the other waitresses were old-fashioned roller skates and short dresses. They're cute, not skimpy in any way but show just enough to get you an extra few bucks in your tip.

It was perfect; I could already see myself working here. One of the waitresses rolled over her name tag said Buttercup, which had me giggle. She took us over to the bar, where we proceeded to order our milkshakes. I chose the double Oreo crunch with whipped cream.

Levi chose the rocky road supreme, which was rocky road ice cream blended with milk she topped with marshmallow which she burned with a mini torch. Then added a dash of whipped cream, almond crumbs, and a cherry.

Levi and I sat patiently, talking about our day and random stuff like our favorite colors and foods. Levi likes the color blue, and his favorite food is fried chicken which I happen to be good at making.

Our milkshakes came, and we slurped them down. I, unfortunately, got a brain freeze while Levi drank his in a solid two minutes and didn't feel a thing.

" Hello Ella, I'm Charles, but everyone here calls me Charlie; when can you start working?" A man said as he came to stand in front of both Levi and me.

Wait, does that mean I got the job? I didn't have an interview or anything? How, well, I'll take what I can get never question a good thing.

"When do you need me?" I smiled sweetly.

CHAPTER ELEVEN

No Kidnapping

I'd like to thank for all the love and support!!!

Levi POV

I've been at the diner for two solid hours watching my queen skate around and take orders. She got the job three days ago and hasn't been happier.

Our connection is growing stronger, and the mating pull is causing me to be a bit on edge. Carter hasn't talked to me so much lately, and neither has Ethan (my delta).

Not only has our connection grown stronger, but I also discovered that Ellie has been living inside a motel. After seeing that, Cody begged me to mark her. He's been trying to breakthrough. At this point, I haven't even let him out to go on a run because I fear he will hunt Ella down and mark her. I have to tell her who I am and who she will be. I planned on doing it in a month, but now it's so urgent I have to break it to her tonight.

"We can kidnap mate. She will love us no matter what."

No, we can not kidnap her, Cody, now; this is why you haven't been let out!

Cody has been agitated. And I don't blame him. I'm eighteen at this age; my father was already mated and married to my mother with me on the way. I know that Ellie's too young to have kids, but that doesn't mean I don't want them.

My beautiful Luna skates up to me with a puzzled look on her face. Her blue doe eyes capture my soul her long lashes blink, and her eyebrows furrow with a question.

"Earth to Levi!!!" She says, waving her hand in front of my face. Her strawberry scent is wafting around me.

"Yes, darling," I reply.

" you've been here for over two hours. Would you like to order something? What about a burger and a shake? Or you can have some ribs. Charlie just finished smoking em out back." She says with her sweet southern tang.

"I'll take it all, including you, my love" at that response, her face turns as red as a rose.

" I don't get a break for another two hours." She whispers in my ear.

"Charlie," I yell as I see his face pop out of the kitchen door. Everyone in the restaurant is probably staring at us, but I don't care. " Sweetheart, here is going on break!" I yell, looking at my girl's name tag. Charlie always gives them sweet or goofy nicknames; he chose sweetheart for my sweetheart.

"No problem!" Charlie calls out.

At this response, I grab Ellie by her waist and hoist her onto my lap. She squeals at this. I stick my head at her neck and start breathing in her sweet scent. I start kissing her neck, looking for the perfect place to mark her. All of a sudden, a moan seeps out of her lips.

"S-s-stop I-t not in p-public," whispers Ellie. I start to growl, well, not me but Cody. Ellie gasps as she turns around and sees my eyes.

"They're their Silver," she gasps, raising her hand to cradle my cheek.

"So beautiful," she sighs, smiling at me. How is she not scared?

Ella

He's a wolf. I'm so in love with him that, and I don't even care.

You're probably wondering how I know he's a werewolf; well, weird story.

Flashback 12years ago

" Hey, there are you lost," said a nice lady; she was short and had long blonde hair and blue eyes. I thought of what my momma must look like. She would be the perfect momma.

I nodded in response to her question and instantly hugged her. She lifted me onto her hip and cradled me while rubbing my back. I'd never been loved like this before; it feels nice. I grab onto her hair and start running my fingers through it. It's long and beautiful.

Then I saw my uncle. He was walking funny, and his face was droopy; I wonder if he drank his magic water again. He walked up to us and was about to yell at my new mommy and me when he suddenly stopped and smiled at her. I looked up to my mommy, and she smiled back.

A week later, she moved in; her name was Annie, and she was a werewolf; she was mated to my uncle. He quit drinking and straightened himself up. She was a beautiful wolf; her coat was light grey, and she'd lay down in the grass of our back yard and let me comb my fingers through her fur and put butterfly clips in her coat. One day Annie went out for a jog, and she never came back.

Uncle Dan began drinking again. This time it was worse; he'd hit me if I were around him. I would cry about my mom, and he'd yell at me, saying she wasn't my real mother, that my mom and dad left me with him and that they didn't love me. He'd forget to feed me. Annie would always provide me, and we'd even make cookies together. She'd ask me if I want other siblings, and I'd always nod. She wanted another kid just like me.

I've never seen a picture of my birth parents, but I've always had a vision of Annie until now. When I ran away, I didn't get the chance to steal the only picture I had left of her. It's a picture of her and me on the swings at the park. I'm smiling at the camera, and she's smiling down at me. She always smiled at me.

~*~*~*~*~*~*~*~*~*~*~*~*~*~*

Werewolves have never threatened me, only have I ever been loved by them. Annie was my only true parent, and she left only after two years.

Looking into his silver eyes, they slowly went back to their brilliant green, and with that, I leaned forward and kissed him. He tried to deepen the kiss, and I pulled away.

" Levi, I work here, remember?" I scold him. He just giggled and pulled me into him and hugged me once again.

"Meet me after work. I'll be sitting here waiting, okay, babe," he whispered in my ear and continued by kissing my neck again. I nod-ded my head, not trusting my voice. After that, I slowly got back up to my feet, trying not to slip while on my skates, and continued my job taking orders and passing out food.

CHAPTER TWELVE

Babies

Ella POV

Like Levi had said, he was still sitting in the corner booth of the diner when my shift was over. I was exhausted, to say the least. I walked over to him, trying to keep my eyes from drooping downward. Levi met me halfway and wrapped me up in a hug. I felt complete bliss standing there in his embrace that before I knew it, I was asleep.

Levi POV

She looked exhausted. I walked up to her and wrapped her in my arms, and I instantly felt her pulse settle and her breathing becomes deep. My sweet angel had fallen asleep in my arms. I lifted her in my arms, told Charlie goodnight, and went to my car. At this point, I was cradling Ellie on my hip. Using my free hand, I opened the car and slowly set her down in the seat. Her face scrunched up when I let her go. Closing her door gently, I went over to my side and buckled both myself and Ella in. Then we were off.

It took about thirty minutes to get home. I soon arrived at the Packhouse and lifted Ellie once again, and headed inside. The Packhouse was spacious. My parents wanted a lot of kids, but my mom wasn't able to, so they were so happy that they could have me.

I headed upstairs to my room. My room was significant; it had big windows that looked outback towards the forest. When I had turned seventeen, my mom redecorated it, claiming that if a lady was to live with me, it had to be suited for one. My bathroom was utterly glamourized by my mother. She even went so far as to put lady products under one of the sinks, holding underneath it a hairbrush, curling stick thingy, and a hairdryer. What grossed me out was that she put condoms at the bottom of my drawer. Thankfully my room was also on the other side of the house from my parents, who gave us more privacy. I closed the door lightly and headed towards the bed. I gently set my angel down and pulled a blanket on her to keep her warm.

I then headed off to take a shower. I walked into the closet, grabbed some sweatpants and a black tee, and headed towards the bathroom.

Ella POV

I felt like I was on a cloud, a very good-smelling cloud. It smelt like Levi, and that's when I decided to shoot my eyes open. I sat up to discover a soft, plush teal blanket draped over me. Looking at my surroundings, I soon realized that I was in the most beautiful room I've ever seen. In front of me were a tiled fireplace and a cabinet which

I assumed held a tv. To my right was a couch that sat right against three large windows, which had a beautiful forest view.I stood up from the bed, and my feet landed on a soft carpet. I quietly walked around the room and opened a door that I assumed led to a bathroom or a closet. It was the closet and a large one at that. I looked inside to find one side full of Levis shoes and the other side empty. The closet was made of dark wood cabinets. As I opened one up, I saw all of Levi's pants and his shirts. On the other side of the closet, where his stuff wasn't, there was a round mirror and racks made for shoes and handbags, along with a seat and makeup desk.

As I turned to walk out, I saw Levi; he was smiling at me, leaning against the closet door frame; his hair was wet. He must have taken a shower.

"Watch a doing in here, babe?" He spoke softly. I smiled back. Not trusting my voice, he walked up to me, put his hands gently on my waist, and leaned forward.

Levi is going to kiss me, my brain screamed. I was so happy I leaned in, and then it happened his lips landed on mine, and my body exploded with joy and pleasure and absolute bliss. His lips were so soft against mine. Levi kisses me gently with so much love and care. As we deepened our kiss, I could feel more emotions reveal themselves, like compassion and need.

"Aww honey, look who Levi brought home" I heard a lady gush as I pulled away from Levi. Who might I say looked annoyed with the woman.

" Mooooom! Really? Now you decide to enter!" Levi wasn't at all happy, but his face was completely red, and he looked cute for being embarrassed.

Before I knew it, I was being pulled out of his hands and then looked at his mother.

" Oh honey, aren't you just the cutest thing on earth. Boy, are you skinny though, well don't worry about that, hun, we'll have to feed you double that way; you guys can make the cutest grandbabies. Oh! I'm so excited to be a grandmother. Oh and dear, you can call me Jane oh wait, no! Call me mom!" She squealed.

" gr- gra- grandbabies. Babies! I'm sixteen! Well, seventeen next Friday, but I'm well I'm not old enough, and I got school?" I stuttered

I look over at Levi, who doesn't even look phased at his mother's mention of babies.

CHAPTER THIRTEEN

Ugly Crying

Levi POV

My mom was obsessed with Ella. After the whole baby talk, she dragged Ellie to our couch to ask her what size she was in, anything clothes-related. She continued to talk to her about babies and baby names which sort of freaked Ella out.

Not too long after, my father walked in and introduced himself. My father can appear intimidating especially considering he's the alpha. I got my looks from my father. My mother and I didn't resemble each other besides our green eyes. Ellie didn't mind meeting my folks; in fact, she seemed pretty happy to have them there.

My dad was impressed by her not being afraid of him. He also laughed at my mother's constant talk of babies.

"Honey their still in school and not ready for children, so stop it with the baby talk you are scaring his poor mate" at the mentioning of the word mate Ella's eyes opened wide as realization dawned on her. I could hear her heartbeat speed up, and her breathing becomes more rapid.

Mom, dad, please leave the room. I mind linked instantly; they left without a word. I ran up to Ella, wrapping her in my arms in an effort to calm her down; her body immediately relaxed, molding into my side.

Ella POV

We're mates. Like Annie was to my uncle. I have a mate. Oh my god. I wasn't sad or angry. I was thrilled. Annie had explained to me that mates are together for life; they love one another and have a family together. That's everything I've ever wanted. Too bad Annie had died. But I knew that deep down, Levi wouldn't leave me.

Looking up into the eyes of the very boy I'd spend the rest of my life with, I felt something that I never felt at home with Dan, and it was unconditional love. I felt complete, and at this, I broke down, crying tears of absolute happiness.

It got to the point where I was full-on ugly crying on my soulmate's lap. I had it all hyperventilating, snot, and tears running down my face. I had puffy eyes and a red face. Levi picked me up and walked into the restroom, setting me down on the beautiful granite counter-top and grabbed a box of tissues, and carefully wiped my face handing me another one to blow my nose.

After my much-needed break down I felt so much better. Looking up into Levi's eyes, I saw them full of worry and concern; at this, I gave him a meek smile.

"I'm okay. They were tears of happiness, not sadness. I'm so grateful I get to be your mate." I told him.

Levi's face lit up with his million-dollar smile. He grabbed me and lifted me from the counter to spin me around.

" Oh, thank goddess, I was worried you wouldn't want me. Cody was getting anxious. And I am happy you want to be with us." He said in a rush.

"Cody?"

" Yes, my wolf, his name is Cody."

" Oh yes, you're wolf. Sorry, it's been a while since I've been around a werewolf." I said in a hushed voice.

At this, Levi gave me a curious look. So I told him about my aunt or who I referred to as my mom. I told him about my family and how they passed away. I told him about my uncle and the abuse, and at this, Levi's eyes turned silver as he stiffened at my words. Telling me, I'm never to go back and that I'm to live here with him. At this, I smiled very pleasedly.

Levi and I talked about anything and everything until we realized that it was dark outside.

We heard a knock at the door. I got up from Levi's lap, which he wasn't too happy about to open the door. To my surprise, there stood Jane with her hands full of shopping bags. She had a grin on her face as he walked past me and to our closet.

" Dear. While you were talking, I took it upon myself to do a little shopping for you. I just got you some clothes," she said sweetly as she walked back out of our room to pick up even more bags and bring them to the closet.

There were so many bags and boxes; full of shoes and accessories, including jewelry and purses, and a new backpack in style. She had bought every shoe know to humanity made for women; there were heels to sneakers and flats. Then there were the clothes. I was surprised that, being an older woman, she knew all the fashion trends.

" Oh my goodness, did you buy out the whole store?" I said with a giggle. Jane just laughed at my comment.

She pulled the clothes out of the bags. They were all from stores I dreamed of shopping at their were Gucci sneakers and Kate Spade handbags. But also more affordable clothes from Abercrombie, American Eagle, Pacsun, and Urban Outfitters. She bought t-shirts and crop tops along with jeans and shorts.

I was in complete and utter shock. I have never had this many clothes in my 16 years of life.

"Sorry If I'm overwhelming you. It's just I've always wanted a daughter, but I was just never able to have one. Thankfully I have you now, so be prepared to be spoiled by Levi and me." She chirped, her eyes held, longing for approval.

I just smiled and walked up to Jane, pulling her into a hug.

" You know I've always wanted a mom. And I'm so glad I have one now," I whispered in her ear. At this, Jane's eyes watered up as she smiled down at me.

"Oh. I nearly forgot dinner should be ready in an hour, dear, so why don't you get washed up and try on some new clothes!" She smiled, walking out of the room. I felt arms wrap around my waist, and the tingles run up and down my spine. I sighed, feeling so happy. And then it hit me. I only have an out to get washed up, and I desperately needed a shower.

" Babe, I need to shower. Do you have a razor or anything I can use that won't make me smell like a boy?" I questioned

" yeah, there should be everything from razors to shampoo under your side of the counter," he said gently in my ear, and at that, I released myself from his grasp. I heard a groan from him once again, upset that I left his embrace.

I walked into the bathroom to see that one side of the sink was full of his cologne and toothbrush. And the other side was empty. As I went over and looked through the drawers, I was pleased to find a razor, cherry blossom shampoo, conditioner, and body wash, along with a few bath bombs, nail polish, women's hygiene products and a pink brand new toothbrush and hairbrush. Boy, did his mom go all out? I grabbed the showering necessities and washed and shaved my body.

I wrapped myself in a towel and headed out to the closet, which at this point was every girl's fantasy.

I chose to wear something nice but somewhat classy for dinner, so I settled on a lovely white button-up long sleeve off-shoulder shirt. And a white embroidered skirt. Once I was done changing, and walked out. I could tell that Levi was pretty pleased with my outfit as he smiled and walked up to and pecked me on the lips. He was looking good himself with his button-down navy blue shirt and a nice pair of jeans; as I looked down, I noticed he was wearing sneakers, and at that, I ran over to the closet and grabbed a couple of heeled sandals was ready to go.

CHAPTER FOURTEEN

Suffocated

Ella POV

When Jane has said dinner, I had expected it just to be Levi, Jane, Max (Levi's father), and I. What I wasn't expecting was his entire family and some of his friends.

I was introduced to everyone. Levi's four aunts had nearly suffocated me with their hugs, and his five uncles were nice enough to give me a handshake. His aunts and uncles had children except for one who I heard haven't found his mate. All in all, about eighty people were sitting at ten different tables set up in their backyard. While some of the younger kids were running around in their bathing suits going in the pool.

I had never gone swimming before. Jane had bought me several bathing suits, but I had never thought they would be handy. Levi was smiling at all his family and held my hand the entire time we were together.

I was bombarded by questions about my age, my grades, how many children I wanted, and my family. I told them the truth when it came to my parents that they died I just left out the whole uncle fiasco. His entire family seemed to become saddened by my response. I told them I wasn't sad that I was lucky to find another family. At this, they all smiled and got back to their chatter and banter.

Jane and all her sisters and sister-in-laws made so much food there was everything, including steak, baked potatoes, and cherry cobbler. I was surprised at the amount of food placed all over the counters in a gourmet fashion.

During our meal, Levi had explained to me how Carter was his beta and his delta Ethan. Carter was the same as ever with his sarcasm and jokes with Levi, but Ethan was more reserved; he would laugh but never really make any jokes, and he'd never look at me in the eyes. It was a bit weird, but I just overlooked it. I was new, and everyone is different in their personalities and attitudes.

After dinner, we had said our goodbyes and hugged everyone. I was glad to be around them; I felt included, and I knew I wasn't all alone anymore.

We walked up the stairs and into our bedroom. I walked into the bathroom without a word, took off my makeup, washed my face, and brushed my teeth. As I placed the brush in its cup holder, I saw Levi walk in and put his hands around my waist. I couldn't help but blush as I saw our reflection in the mirror. It was somewhat comical. Our height difference was astounding.

Turning around in his arms, I hugged my giant in response. Levi picked me up and hugged me.

" Hey Ellie, we need to talk." He whispered in my ear. I nodded my head. Most girls would be worried about their boyfriend saying, 'they needed to talk,' but I wasn't. I knew that Levi was my mate, and he couldn't leave me without feeling pain.

Levi gently set me down afterward. He grabbed my hairbrush off the counter and walked me over to the bed. I sat on the end with my legs dangling off the side as Levi sat behind me and started to gently brush through all my tangles.

"So... I just wanted to talk to you about the whole Luna position you're going to have as my mate." He said.

"Okay, well, what am I going to be doing?" I questioned, somewhat worried for his response.

" Well, you will meet the entire pack and be a sort of mother figure. You know, help out when needed may have to help with the pack paperwork. My mom will probably have you cook also?" He said, sounding worried about my response. All in all, it sounded pretty good to me. I liked being around children and helping out, I also loved cooking, and I have always been terrific in school, so I wasn't too worried about paperwork.

"Okay, sounds nice. I can't wait to meet the rest of the pack," I replied confidently.

Levi let out a long sigh. I hadn't even realized that he had been holding in. I turned around on the bed, facing him and putting both my palms up to his face. His eyes shined with adoration and care at this. I smiled and lightly pecked him on his lips; even at the slight and fast kiss, I could still feel the electricity got through my body.

I leaned back, jumped off the bed, and hurried into the closet to grab some pajamas. I settled on a pair of pajama shorts that were plain but had a silk texture and were the color black and wandered off to Levi's side of the closet. After snooping around, I found what I was looking for and grabbed one of his Nike t-shirts. It was grey and had a white logo on it. It was too big on me, landing mid-thigh. I walked out into the bedroom to see Levi lying on the bed in just a pair of boxers. His abs on full display, I just stopped and stared at the Greek god in front of me, not believing my eyes. He was all mine, no one else's. Levi instantly noticed me ogling him.

" Like what you see? Angel." He asked with a smirk.

" Yes. Do you like what you see?" I responded, putting one hand on my hip and the other on my head in a fashion pose.

At this, Levi started laughing until he was gasping for air. I stayed in the pose until he was finished, still waiting for his reply. And once he was done, he started shaking his head, repeating yes about four times, at which I stopped, hopped on the bed, and snuggled into his chest, enjoying this moment and hoping that it would last.

Levi

Ellie had just fallen asleep when Carter's mind linked me.

"Theirs a pup at the border. He came from a neighboring pack he's injured!" Carter said frantically.

"We're coming," I responded.

"Ellie. Wake up. You need to be a Luna now." Ella instantly got up, looking at me, hearing my concern laced in my voice.

"What's wrong," she asked, getting up from the bed.

" I'll tell you on the way, put on some jeans and a T-shirt," I said, walking towards the closet to grab my clothes with her.

CHAPTER FIFTEEN

Little Girl

Levi POV

We got changed in a rush and started are walk down towards the pack hospital. Ella has finally seen part of the pack houses which she gasped in awe. Our packs houses weren't small everyone had a fairly large house and we all lived in a gated community to prevent outsiders from coming in. The forest was connected to the community through a large entry way but was all private property.

Once we arrived to the hospital we rushed into the child's room. Their in the hospital bed was a three year old girl. She laid in the bed with a bruised face and with her right arm broken. She had blonde hair and pale skin. I could feel the power radiating off her she must have been the alpha's daughter.

Sensing someone their she opened her eyes slowly squinting as she adjusted to the light. Her eyes were blue and similar to my Lunas with the exception that they were slightly brighter in color. She weakly smiled at the sight of Ella being beside me.

Ella slowly walked up to her and pulled a chair up to the side of her bed.

" Why hello their sugar. I'm Ella but you can call me Ellie." She said sweetly introducing herself to the child. The little girl giggled at Ellie.

" I'm Adaline and I'm three years old how old are you?" She asked curiously.

" I'm 16 years old and I'm going to be seventeen in a little over a week. Where did you come from?" At Ellie's question Adaline's face morphed into a frown as tears threatened to fall down her sweet face.

"I'm from the MoonBlood pack. M-my Mommy and Daddy died." She cried. In response to this Ella lifted the girl off the bed and cradled her in her arms. Saying sweet things in her ear. This hushed Adalines crying into soft sniffing.

"Her fathers Alpha Eric and her mother's Luna Sophia. They were both are or were 21" I mumbled loud enough for Ella to hear.

Adaline had fallen asleep in Ella's arms and she slowly placed her in the bed and pulled me out of the room into the hallway.

Ella

I couldn't believe it that sweet angle was left all alone to fend for herself. How could this have possibly happened?

" Levi what are we to do? What happened to her family?" I asked in a hush tone not wanting to wake up the child in the room next to us.

" I don't know what we're going to do. She's probably going to have to live with us considering she's an Alphas child. Her pack was likely taken down by rogues they were very small." He said in response. This broke my heart.

They were so young her parents. Their family was just starting. All was left of their family was Adaline. I couldn't help but start to cry. I know crying won't fix thing but I can't help it.

Levi wrapped me in his arms. I started hearing crying coming from in Adalines room I rushed in to see her turning in her bed tears running down her face she's having a nightmare I picked her up gently making sure not to hurt her armed and cradled her until the tears stopped running down her face.

I knew at that moment I wanted her. I wanted her to be my own. Looking up to Levi he could tell by the expression on my face that no matter what he said he wasn't going to take this child away from me.

I know I'm just sixteen, but I couldn't leave her and she'd end up being with us no matter what.

Levi's face didn't show fear or anxiety at the thought of being a parent to Adaline. Instead it showed pure happiness.

Levi

I was so happy I knew that Ellie wasn't ready to physically have a child although she was already ready to be a mother to Adaline. I knew my mother was going to be so happy she wants grandchildren no matter what.

"Mom I'm bringing home a grandchild you're going to be a grand-ma. I need you to prepare the room next to the nursery into a little girls room." I mind linked her. She'd probably be a bit upset that I woke her up , but once she hears grandma she'll be fine.

"I'm going to be a grandma! I'll wake up your father it will take us all day tomorrow to get her room ready son" she linked back.

I knew that our little family was growing and would continue to grow.

Ellie looked up at me with the biggest smile on her face. Out of tragedy their can sometimes be miracles. Our daughter was a miracle.

Ella

After two days Adaline was released and going home with us. I had spent every minute with her. Thankful that it was the weekend. I hadn't missed any school.

Jane has come in and we came up with the plan to have her take care of Adaline while we were at school and once we got home she was ours for the rest of the day. I also told them that I'd take a free period so I'd have the morning with Adaline and take Levi's Jeep to school.

When we got home Adalines face was in complete shock at the size of our home. But after looking up at us her face became more calm and we walked her inside and took her on a tour. Jane has told us what room she was in as we walked her into her room she squealed running around and looking at everything. I have to admit that Jane did a real number on the room it was every little girls dream and instantly brought a pure smile to Adalines face. The room was completely decked out with a princess theme which included dresses for her to wear. Along with a play kitchen and doll house.

I turned to look at Levi's reaction to the room and even he seemed surprised.

" My moms always wanted a little girl. Now she's got two" he whispered in my ear.

Chapter Sixteen

Calculus

Ella POV

A week has past since Adaline became part of our family. Levi and his father Max had connections with child services and we were able to adopt without any trouble.

Addy has finally settled down into our house and enjoys her room and her new grandparents. We had found out that a group of rogues had attacked her pack and burned down the entire place. Their were only ten other survivors who we gladly offered to join our pack.

I had finally gone to the counselors office to get my first period changed into a free period. Because of my grades they allowed me to take my first period off and switch my periods around.

Levi wasn't happy with my schedule change and went up to the office to also get his classes changed into all of mine. I was surprised that he ended up in all my classes except my free period. The his counselor was apparently part of our pack and was a willing to change his classes.

Levi's possessiveness has increased greatly. It's kinda cute in a way when we went back to school he growled at every guy who looked my way. Jane said it will continue to increase until he marks me. The thought of the marking process honestly scares me a little.

I woke up to the beginning of the school week. Our alarm went off at 6:30 so Levi is awake for school and it also gives me time to hang out with Addy before I have to go. I have to go to work today so I want spend as much time as I can with her.

Levi's arms were wrapped around me spooning me in our bed. He was a deep sleeper where as I'm a very light sleeper. I tried to get out of his hold unsuccessful might I add. This man is made of steel I swear.

" Babe, it's time to wake up" I cooed in his ear. His eyes slowly opened and he started smiling at me. Leaning in I gave him a kiss surprising him enough to loosen his hold. I unwrapped him from around me and headed to the shower. It took me about ten minutes to bathe and brush my hair and teeth. I walked in the closet to put on my outfit for the day I decided on some blue shorts and a light creamy yellow button up crop top. And to finish the look I chose to wear some brownish beige booties which I'd put on when I'd leave for school.

I walked in to Addy's room to find her fast asleep on her bed laying on her belly. She was the cutest thing. Like Levi she was also a very heavy sleeper. Her nightmares have begun to stop she gets them not as often which is a relief. When she was in the hospital she had gotten them often now in our home not so much. I quietly walked over to her bed and sat on the edge and rubbed her back in order to wake her up.

" Hey baby girl, its time to wake up. Do you want some pancakes for breakfast?" I offered at the mention of food Addy sat up instantly her blonde hair was disheveled in her princess nightgown. I lifted her up from the bed and carried her to her restroom. She brushed her teeth as I braided her hair into a French braid. Afterwards we went into her closet to grab her an outfit for today.

" I want to look like you." She stated. I giggled at her remark and grabbed a yellow blouse and a jean skirt from her closet. Once she was dressed she spun around in her mirror happy with her outfit. With that we headed off to the kitchen.

I pulled out the pancake mix, bacon and eggs from the fridge. And started making our food. Addy started talking about anything that came to her mind. When I was in the middle of making the pancakes I heard a question I hadn't expected come from Adaline.

"Are you my new Mommy?" She asked simply as if her question wasn't a big deal. I placed the fully cooked pancake on a plate and added butter on the top, placing bacon and eggs on the side of the plate. I walked over to Addy putting the plate in front of her and sat next to her.

"Adaline would you like me to be your mom?" I questioned hopefully.

" Yes I want you to be my new momma and Mr. Levi my daddy" I smiled at this and lifted Adaline from her seat into a hug. I started to cry of pure happiness.

"Yes baby girl. I'd love to be your new momma"

Levi came running down the stairs in response to me crying. I placed Addy back in her seat before walking over to hug Levi. After my much needed hug I dragged him over to a nearby room to share my latest conversation with our daughter.

Levi's face lit up at my news. He was just as happy with the news as I was. We have officially gotten what we wanted Addy to want us as her parents.

Levi POV

Ellie and I had a great morning and so was the beginning of school for today. I waited outside calculus for Ella to arrive at school. I saw her walk through the entrance doors of our school. She instantly spotted me immediately walking towards me when she was stopped by a boy.

I knew who he was because I've seen him around. His name was Eddie he had blonde hair and wasn't muscular. Cody wasn't happy with another guy wanting to be around or with our mate.

" Don't let him near her she is ours. Protect mate." Cody growled.

I often disagree with Cody but this time I can say that we were both on the same page. I stormed up to Ella and wrapped my arms around her waist protectively. At this she started to giggle. I don't know what she found so funny about her talking to another guy.

"James this is my overly possessive boyfriend, Levi. Levi this is James. James how's you're boyfriend?" She asked giggling even more and at this point so was James. I had made a mistake big deal no matter what he was a guy.

"He's great. We're going on a date later today." The Eddie kid replied.

They continued to chat for the next three minutes before we said our goodbyes and walked into our class. Most of our classmates were already seated although some kids were still loitering around and talking to one another. This was one of the classes where we don't sit together. Ellie sits in the front of the class next to some guy named Ralph and Avery. While I'm seated three rows behind her.

Mr. Burns started his lecture. I was writing down the notes on the bored when I saw Ralph lean in and whisper into my mates ear. What the hell does he think he's doing. Ellie turned to him and gave him a face of pure disgust and within a second her hand had slapped him right across his face. That was definitely going to leave a mark.

"Yes!" I yelped. With pride that's my love!

Which made the entire class laugh along with Ellie's act of aggression. Luckily our teacher didn't see her slap Ralph so she was never sent to the office or anything. I however got a stern talking to by Mr. Burns after class.

Ella

Once Levi got out of class. I grabbed his hand and entwined our fingers together. I instantly felt calmer at the feeling of our sparks.

Ralph had asked me if I wanted to feel how it is true be with a real man. I couldn't help it but hit him. The way he disrespected my mate had me seeing red. If there wasn't a class full of students I probably would have punched him or kicked him where the sun dot shine.

Levi wanted to know what had happened but I instantly shut that conversation down. I told him we'd discuss it later tonight. Although if love for Levi to beat up Ralph I also whatevs him to stay at our school and graduate.

Changing the conversation we talked about Addy and we agreed that she'd come visit me at work with Levi. It's so sweet that he can sense when I'm upset or want something.

My birthday is tomorrow and I can't help but wonder what he's going to do. I haven't celebrated my birthday since Anna was still with my uncle. She had thrown me a big party and had some of my kindergarten friends over. We had a piñata and an ice cream cake. That was one of my happiest memories.

"Hey what's wrong" Levi asked turning me to him. I hadn't even realized their were tears running down my face.

I quickly wiped them away. We had five minutes in between periods and I told him about my fifth birthday party.

The rest of our morning classes went by in a breeze we sat next to each other in every class except calculus. I walked up to Avery's locker and we walked into the cafeteria together with Levi on our trail. Today's lunch was greasy pizza which in my opinion was a bit better than the chicken sandwich. Levi had insisted I'd pack a lunch at home but I refused if Avery had to eat Cafeteria food the. I would to. We grabbed our food and sat under our tree.

Levi had brought cookies from home that I had baked with Addy or more like I baked them and she ate the dough. He passed around the cookies. Carter swallowed his whole as Avery ate hers carefully the same as I did.

"Avery you should come to the diner tonight. You can eat whatever you want on the house." I asked. Avery's eyes got wide with joy but was gone in an instant.

" I don't think I can I have to take care of my little sister and brother tonight." She stated sadly.

"The more the marrier!" I smiled brightly at her at this she nodded and agreed to join us tonight. Levi also invited Carter and we all decided to have dinner together at the end of my shift.

Levi

I headed home as Ella headed to the diner. I had walked through the door and was suddenly tackled to the floor by Addy.

"Well hey their angel. How was your day?" I questioned her.

Addy told me about her day and all the things that my mom has done with her what hit me was the last statement she said.

" oh and grandma took me to the mall and we got me earrings they are so sparkly!" She said excitedly. I couldn't believe my mother put holes through my daughters ears and without me their!

" Thats nice baby, I'll be back in a second how about you draw me a picture?" Addy nodded and with that I hunted down my mom.

She was on the couch in our upstairs library shopping no doubt online for either her, Ellie, or Addy. She saw me stomp in and froze like a deer stuck in the headlights.

"You put holes in my daughter's ears!" I growled.

"Now Levi don't you dare speak to me like that!"

" Mom what do you think Ella's going to say to you? How could you do this. This is a milestone you shouldn't have done this!" I stated

" Honey I think your being a bit dramatic. Plus she loves them. She chose out the color earring she wanted." My mother responded

I couldn't deal with this right now so I decided to just calm down and spend the rest of my day with Addy until it was time to leave to see Ella.

CHAPTER SEVENTEEN

Big Girl

Ella POV

My shift wasn't to hard today although we were busy I was getting better at working at the diner. I was now able to roller skate with ease and get everyone their orders correct. Charlie said I was doing great which made me smile. My shift should be over in about fifteen minutes. As I had just finished placing some of our costumers plates down at their table I saw Levi enter the diner with Addy on his hip.

I smiled and waved and returned to my tasks asking the family I was serving if they needed anything else they all responded no. But I couldn't help but grab an extra napkin for the baby boy covered in ketchup eating his chicken strips. The mother thanked me and with that I headed off to the kitchen to grab the other tables orders. I had finished my shift and headed over to the bathroom with my bag in hand and changed into my outfit from school.

I saw both Levi and Addy sitting in a bigger booth than our usual one. As I sat down Addy came up and sat right next to me leaning her head into my side. I couldn't help but see something sparkle through her hair. Brushing the strands behind her ear with my fingers I saw a pink diamond stud pierced in her ear.

" I see you got your ears pierced today. Did it hurt or were you a big girl" I said smiling down at her.

" I was a big girl. It hurt just a little bit but I'm fine. Grandma even let me pick out the color." She said beaming at me with a full blown smile.

I could see Levi wasn't to happy about his mothers decision. But I gave him a reassuring smile hoping he'd understand that it's okay. A minute later Avery walked through the door with her little brother and sister. Her sister was about ten years old and her brother five. They both greeted us and sat down. We introduced Adaline to Avery as my daughter. Addy looked similar to me with her having blue eyes and her pale skin.

Avery's eyes grew wide probably assuming that Addy was genetically mine. And although we didn't have the same blood I didn't correct her for her misunderstanding either. Addy was mine. Well and Levi's to. Carter showed up three minutes later and gave Addy a bright smile which made her giggle.

" Whats up cupcake?" He asked Addy. In which she responded by telling him all about her day with grandma and Levi. She also showed him her newly pierced ears complements of grandma.

Addy loved Carter. Carter brought her treats whenever he came over from ice cream to a Barbie doll. Giving him the title of Uncle C.

We all ordered our food the children settled for chicken strips, Avery and I ordered the cheeseburger mine with fries, and hers with fruit salad. Levi got the ribs and Carter got the roast beef sandwich. Everyone ordered a shake on the side except for Carter who got a root beer float.

When we finished eating Levi payed the bill and we all said our goodbyes and headed home. Adaline was exhausted and fell asleep within seconds of being buckled into her car seat. Adaline was small for her age. That was something Levi and I had noticed once we adopted her. Apparently she was a premature baby which makes her smaller than most wolfs. Adaline had made it to our borders alive which hadn't made much sense since she still hasn't shifted. We came to believe she may have been dropped off by a rogue. Which makes us question what do they want?

We arrived at the house as the sun was going down. It was 6:00 making Adalines bedtime in two hours. She woke up as we lifted her out of her car seat and walked into the house. We decided on watching a movie before going to bed. We watched Tangled and painted our toes. Addy loved the color pink. So I painted them a sparkly pink.

Once the movie had ended Adaline was asleep cuddling into my side. I turned the tv off and picked her up. I woke her up to brush her teeth as I undid her braid and redid it so her hair wasn't a mess tomorrow morning. She put her pajamas on and I tucked her in. Turning on her nightlight I left the room. Levi was doing his paperwork in his office.

I walked in to him being hunched over her desk signing forms and making calculations.

"Hey, do you need any help?" And with that I was put to work doing calculations for the company and the pack. We finished in an hour and headed up to our room. I put on a silk nightgown I found in my closet and some underwear on. Grabbing a ponytail from the bathroom put my hair up into a large bun. Levi was laying on the bed waiting for me to join him.

He groaned as he saw me leave the bathroom causing a blush to run up my neck onto my cheeks. I crawled on to the bed and snuggled into his side. We talked about what happened at school this morning at the mention of Ralph he became stiff, and then with me telling him what he said Levi growled.

I got up and straddle Levi within an instant. His eyes were full of lust at my sudden actions. I leaned down and kissed him. Sparks flew through my body and Levi threw me down on the bed as we continued our make out session with him on top of me. His lips left mine as he trailed kisses down my jaw onto my neck. He continued to kiss and suckle my neck until he found the spot that made me moan and then he pulled away.

I knew he wanted to mark me and with a quick nod giving him permission he went back to my neck and as I moaned again I felt his teeth scratch at the surface of my skin and then sink in. I let out a yelp at the pain but as soon as it was their it was replaced by pure and utter bliss. Levi licked my neck at the spot he had marked me. And we went back to kissing. His tongue trailed the seem of my lips asking for entry. I refused and in response he nipped at my bottom lip making me gasp at this he took his chance and slipped his tongue in making us moan. His tongue fought for dominance winning. We pulled apart both of us breathing heavily. Our foreheads leaning against one another. With one last peck Levi rolled over next to me and pulled me to him. And within a matter of seconds we were asleep.

Beep. Beep. Beep. Our alarm went off. Wow my pillow smells really good. I thought I opened my eyes to see I was wrapped around Levi laying on top of him. As I tried to get up he pulled me to him nuzzling my neck. Boy was he not a morning person. I then remembered the events that occurred last night and began to blush. Oh god. It's official I have a mate.

"Yes you do Happy Birthday love." Levi said in my head.

"Aaaah" I screamed

Levi shot up in our bed and inspected me to see if I was hurt or not.

"W-what j-just h-happened!" I stuttered in shock.

Levi

" Oh I'm sorry. We can talk through our link. We can mind link because, we, well I marked you.

She seemed a bit confused but after explaining it she seemed fine. Today was my angels birthday.

"Happy Birthday!" Yell Addy running into our room with my mom on her trail. Addy hopped on the bed and jumped into Ella's arms.

"Why thank you" she said back with a smile on her face. In my moms hand was a tray of waffles with whipped cream and strawberries on top.

My moms eyes dropped down to Ella's neck which my mark was in full view. It was beautiful my mark had transformed into a crescent moon it was simple but engraved at the edge of the moon was our names hooked together by an infinity sign. I couldn't help but smile at it.

After we ate breakfast I told Ella to put her bathing suit on and an outfit over it. I said the same to Addy who waited for Ella to finish getting dressed so Ella could help her. Apparently I have no fashion sense according to my love and our baby.

I hadn't planned on going to school today because of Ella's birthday so instead I was flying the girls out to California to spend a couple days by the beach. I called the companies captain a couple days ago to tell him our plans and we set up the date. My mom had packed the Ella a suitcase and Addy a duffle bag. I packed my own bag while Ellie was at work so it could be a surprise. Ellie has moved from Tennessee to Arkansas and from what I've heard she's never. Been to the beach and neither has Addy.

Ella

I don't know why Levi's so excited I can't swim. I took a shower before I got dressed making sure to shave. I washed my hair and body after I had gotten out of the shower I put my hair up in a towel to dry off as I brushed my teeth. What I hadn't expected was to see my mark. It was beautiful once I saw our names on it I started to cry. After my little happy tears sesh. I put my hair up in to French braids that ended at the base of my head and let my hair flow down my back. My mark was visible for all to see.

I walked into the closet and went through the bathing suits I had and found a cute blue one with a yellow rose floral design and high waisted shorts which showed a little booty. I'm guessing Levi wouldn't enjoy other people seeing me in. Oh well.

It took me a while to find a cute outfit to go over my suit. It was a greenish dress which I paired with teal sandals and cute little purse. It was kind of short but I wouldn't be wearing it long if we were going in the pool.

After I was done I walked out and picked up Addy placing her on my hip. Walking out of the room before Levi could say a word about my dress.

We walked into Addy's room and over to her closet Addy talked about how her and grandma made our breakfast. I listened to every word she said as we picked out her outfit. We decided on floral shorts and a shirt set with a matching headband. We put her in the bath and after she was cleaned up we brushed her hair braiding it into her

Underneath we put on her bathing suit on her which was pink tankini with shiny gold unicorn pattern on it.

Once we were finished we walked down the hall to my room as I entered to find Levi sitting on the couch by the window in a pair of swim trunks and fitted T-shirt which complemented his muscles. He looked up from his phone to smile at both of us. He can up to me and kissed my on the cheek picking up Addy and whispering in her ear making her giggle.

"What are y'all talking about?" I say with a smirk on my face this had Addy giggling more.

Levi set her down and she ran from our room and back with a package wrapped in festive birthday paper with a bow on the top and a card. The box wasn't too big in fact it was on the small side never the less I grabbed the box with a thank you and opened the card.

It was home made and so cute. It had a stick figure drawing of our small family and written above was happy birthday in Levi's hand writing. I opened it to find another picture that Addy drew with her and I and a bunch of balloons it was signed by Adaline and her messy but perfect hand writing.

I bent down to give her a big hug telling her how much I loved the card and then went on to open the box. Inside was a brand new phone. My old phone didn't really work and I guess Levi noticed it was the latest IPhone it came with AirPods and a portable charger which was pink in fact everything was put in light pink cases that had sparkles. No doubt my little girl picked it out herself.

" Why thank you. I love the pink and glitter." I said pulling on Levi's shirt so he could kiss me and then turning and pecking Addy on the cheek.

Levi

I had to get her a phone which also had a tracking device placed inside which I whispered into Ellie's ear explaining its just for protection because of the rogues.

We headed outside to the Jeep. After buckling up Addy in the back and opening the passenger door for Ellie I got in the drivers side and we headed off toward the airport. Listening to Ella's music which consisted of the Beatles and The Beach Boys.

I had set the alarm a five this morning so we'd be out around 6:30 which I was pleasantly surprised that we were out at 6:40. My girls are good at not taking forever to get dressed. Our flight will be long. We should get to our destination around 6 hours so we should make it their around two in the afternoon with enough time to spend the rest of our day at the beach relaxing.

When we pulled up to the airport Ella's eyes lit up she hopped out of the car around to Addy and lifted her out of the car seat. Placing her on her feet. Because of how small Adaline is she still uses a stroller mostly because of how easily tired she gets.

I got to the trunk and took out our bags and placed her stroller down. After we buckled her in I grabbed the bags as Ellie pushed Addy through the airport.

We are young very young to be parents so most older women that past us just gave us dirty looks because we had a child most of these looks were made towards Ella who was oblivious to them putting all her focus on our little girl.

Once we got to the scanning station the stroller was checked and Addy was lifted into Ellie's arms. They both walked through the detector and after I came through we put our shoes back on grabbing our bags and headed toward our plane. Since it was a private plane we had to go the FBO terminal. After arriving we gave them our names and info and were boarded onto the plane.

It was a nice plane. It had couches and four chairs set up around a table, along with a bar, and television setup on the wall. We sat down placing Addy's car seat on one of the chairs buckling her in. I left the seat next to her empty so Ella could sit next to our daughter and I across. Once we were all settled I couldn't help but smile at my girls they were sitting there holding hands and talking about random stuff waiting for our flight to take off.

Our attendant went over flight protocol afterwards she proceeded to take our orders I just stared at my angels as I was about to order my drink I saw Ella's face morph into a scowl towards the lady. I looked over to the lady taking our order and found a blonde lady blatantly checking me out in front of my mate and our child. Before I could even call her out Ella stood up and did something I never would have expected....

Chapter Eighteen

Angel

Ella POV

I was so happy sitting here with my little girl and the love of my life when that blonde fake ass bimbo walked up to get our orders. Now I'm not usually one to judge but she just gave off a bad vibe and when she started checking out my mate. I couldn't stand it.

I stood up shocking Levi and turned to the lady. Pushing her on the shoulder to get her attention. She turned to me giving me a look of disgust. At that point I was completely done this bitch has to go.

"Levi put you hands over Addy's ears"

Levi jumped up from his seat running around us in record time covering our sweet daughters ears.

"Do you know who I am" I asked sweetly towards the tramp.

At my tone her face turned to a sneer. Right as she was about to respond I cut her off.

" Oh. I'm sorry of course you don't know who I am. Why, I haven't introduced myself. I'm Ella his fiancé and that over their is our daughter. Isn't she cutest." I stated laying on my accent thick.

The attendants face still shows disgust.

"I thought you were just some hick he was slumming with." She snaps.

At that moment I did something that I shouldn't be proud of but it was necessary. I slapped her across her makeup caked face and might I say it felt good.

Behind me I heard Levi laughing at my actions. He stood behind me wrapping his hands around my waist. Pulling my body fully against his.

"You bit.." before she could finish it Levi cut her off.

" This is my future wife. You will not speak to her or my daughter like that or I will make sure you can't find a job in the future. I suggest you button up your shirt and get the hell off my plane." At his stern words the lady's face broke into sob as she ran off the plane.

I turned to see Addy wearing earbuds watching Frozen oblivious to what had just occurred. I couldn't help but laugh. I just slapped some random bitch and got away with it.

We went back to our seats and this time Levi asked me what I'd like to drink I asked for a sprite and a juice box for Addy. Levi came back with our drinks and some potato chips and then are plane went off.

It was my first time flying but I wasn't too worried in fact I took the take off fairly well. About an hour after we took off I fell asleep and was woken up a little over an hour later because well someone had to go to the ladies room after a quick trip to the bathroom. We sat back down in our seats Levi was asleep in the seat across from me with one hand on his chest and the other still holding some potato chips he was going to eat before he passed out. I pulled my phone out and took a picture of him setting it as my home screen.

As time passed Addy and I had finished two other Disney movies when the pilot announced we'd be landing in less than thirty minutes. The announcement didn't even wake Levi up and Addy was just excited for us to land. Levi refused to tell me where we were landing so although I knew we were somewhere else I didn't know where.

The plane started landing and once we were on the ground Levi woke up to the shaking of the plane hitting the runway.

"We have now landed in California" the pilot stated. We were in California.

Looking out the window I could only see a few palm trees everything else was runway and random planes. Unbuckling Addy and standing up we grabbed our bags and headed out of the plane and into the airport. Levi had finally gotten the stroller from the pilot and after it was set up Addy was placed inside.

The airport was huge. It was larger than the last airport and was filled with so many people I was thankful that Addy was in a stroller That way she wouldn't get lost if she let go of my hand. We walked through the airport with Levi next to me the whole time.

I noticed the older ladies giving me dirty looks for having Addy. I didn't enjoy them judging Levi and I. Although I couldn't do anything to change it I just prayed that Adaline never noticed it. We finally reached the car rental and after ten minutes Levi returned with the keys to our ride.

Levi had gotten us a Porsche Cayenne SUV. The car was a beautiful blue. After opening the trunk and placing all our bags in Levi came over to put the stroller away while I buckled Addy up. Once we were all inside Levi drove off. I couldn't believe my eyes their were palm trees all around us and beach shops and to our right was the ocean. After a good thirty minutes we pulled into a nice neighborhood right next to the beach. Levi said that we were in Carlsbad right by San Diego. The House wasn't as big as the pack house however it was still a really large house. We opened the doors grabbed all our stuff and walked into a beautiful boho styled house.

Levi dropped our stuff off into our rooms and now we are headed towards the beach. I'd never seen the ocean except for in pictures and books but seeing it in person was just amazing. It one of the most beautiful things I've ever seen besides my mate and our little girl of course. We stayed at the beach for about two hours building sand castles searching for shells and splashing each other with water. Adaline loved the beach she was upset when it was time to go inside but after Levi promised we'd come back tomorrow she went back to being her cheery self. Once we got inside we took showers to get all the sand and salt off our bodies.

Levi announced that we were going down to the board walk tonight and to get dressed. I changed once again into a dark green off the shoulder long sleeve shirt with a denim skirt. Pairing it with hoops placing my hair in a high ponytail that went down my back I was going to wear sandals but second guessed myself knowing that we'd be walking and settled for some white adidas.

Satisfied with the result I walked into Addy's room to see Levi trying to help her find an outfit.

" What about this you like the color pink?" Levi cooed trying his best for her to say yes.

"No!" Addy yelled getting really worked up. Levi looked crushed. Although he really wanted to be successful the likelihood was slim to none.

"Adaline don't yell it's unladylike and rude!" I scolded. Adaline's face showed a bit of fear proving that I had got the message across walking into her closet I pulled out a T-shirt and some pink floral shorts that I thought looked good together and grabbed her sandals knowing that Levi would probably carry her for the night.

Adaline put on her outfit without any hesitation making Levi's jaw drop. Once she was done putting her shoes on we walked into the restroom to do her hair. I put her hair in high pig tails and placed two pearl Bobby pins in her hair to add a bit of style. Once I was finished we started walking out to the car and locked the doors on the way out.

The boardwalk wasn't very far from the house. We parked about a block away. Levi places Addy on his shoulders putting one hand behind her back to support her and the other held mine. I took a picture at that moment. Addy has her hands placed on Levi's forehead as she held on. The walk was nice. I loved holding onto Levi's hand.

"Hey. Babe. Just wanted to say that it was really sexy watching you slap that attendant earlier". Levi linked me making me double over and laugh. I still can believe I did that.

When we arrived at the board walk it was full of rides, food, games, and attractions it was very similar to a fair. We walked around looking at everything. Levi stopped us at one of the games it was the High Striker (this is the game with the hammer and the bell). After paying the man he handed me Addy. We watched as Levi hit the plate with the wooden hammer. The bell went off as the guy asked which prize Levi would like to choose.

Even though the prizes ranged from big fluffy bears to small candies he chose the perfect prize. It was a simple medium sized pink bear which had a pink bow tied around its neck. Levi turned to me and gave me the bear kissing me on the lips. It was sweet and simple.

"Is this our first date?" I linked Levi catching him off guard. This is the first time that I have ever mind linked him intentionally.

" Well yes and no? I had planned for this before Adaline's adoption so intention wise yes?" He questioned his answers making me giggle. It's nice to know that even though it was supposed to be our first date that he still included Adaline.

" Then it's our first date." I replied smiling up at him squeezing his hand in reassurance.

We decided to head over to a cotton candy booth where we bought some pink cotton candy to share. Addy was so happy for the candy sadly her fingers got all stick and pink sugar residue was left all over

Levi's hair and forehead. This had me taking once again another picture.

Adaline was to young to go on any of the rides so instead we played games and ate some shaved ice. Adaline played a duck game and won a cat beanie baby which she just loved. Eventually we got tired and decided it was time to leave and head back home.

We stopped at a burger joint called In-N-Out. The drive through was extremely busy and although the inside also looked busy Levi said it should be quicker. As we walked inside I was welcomed with the smell of burgers and fries. I moaned at the smell which had Levi growling.

Levi

Cody has been a bit on edge today I had a blast with my girls at the boardwalk we ate sweets and played games. Although Cody wasn't something has been bugging him and when I try to confront him he won't tell me what's wrong.

We walk into the restaurant and then Ellie moans at the smell of food I let out an accidental growl. It just happens sometimes. Ella giggles at me leaning up and kissing me on the cheek.

"Okay who wants food because I'm starving. Addy what do you want?" Ella asks.

Adaline was tired we could all tell she just wanted to go to bed and it was a little over an hour past her bed time.

"I want food." Addy replied snuggling more into Ella's side playing with her hair as we waited in line. I chuckled a Addy's response.

When we got up to the register Ella started ordering off what she wanted.

" I'll have a cheeseburger no onions, and a cup of water. Then we'll get another cheeseburger with only lettuce on it. Babe what do you want" she asked turning to me.

" I'll have the double cheeseburger with everything on it and a medium drink."

Once we finished our order we got our slip and headed over to a newly cleaned table and sat down. Ella and I treated today as our date we asked each other random questions and learned new stuff about each other. I learned that Ella hates coleslaw and loves French fries. Her favorite show is Shitts Creek and her favorite book is   Harry Potter and the Prisoner of Azkaban.

We finished our food rather quickly and drove home. When we arrived Adaline was asleep and Ella wasn't far off we got out of the car I carried Addy up to the house with Ella at my side. Once we got inside we walked upstairs. Ella took Addy and walked into her room I headed to the bathroom taking a quick shower and put on some boxers and a T-shirt. I walked back to Adaline's room to check up on my girls Ella was tucking our baby in. Adalines hair was wet from her shower. I walked over to her and kissed her on the head wishing our angel a good night.

Ella walked into the bathroom and took a shower. She was exhausted I could tell. Once she was done the door opened and out walked my love. She was dressed in a pair of white pajamas which had black polka dots. She was gorgeous, her hair was up on the top of her hair in a big bun. She walked over and climbed in bed next to me and curled into my side. And then we fell asleep.

CHAPTER NINETEEN

Traitor

Levi POV

I woke up to crying. I'm a deep sleeper so to have it wake me up is a big deal. Rubbing my eyes Ella was no where in our room. The crying started to subside following the whimpering down the hall. I opened Addy's room to see Ella cradling her as Addys tears soaked through Ella's shirt. Walking into the room Adaline looks up and what I saw nearly broke my heart. She was so scared at what she had seen. Her face was red and splotchy with tear stained cheeks.

The worst part that worries me the most was the letter attached to the window next to her bed.

If it was this easy to scare you I wonder how easy it be to kill you? Tell your mate Happy Birthday for me.-Anon

He or she's who wrote it does scare me and it kills me to know someone came into our house while I was present and scared my child. Whatever sick bastard this was is going to get it.

Ellie and I return to our room with Adaline. I promise to stay awake as they sleep and assure Ella that we will be cutting our vacation short to return to our pack.

I stayed awake as I promised Ella was next to me with Addy curled up next to her. I knew that whoever this was wasn't going to break my family. I would die for my family than have anyone hurt them.

Ella

WI woke up early and packed up our belongings with Levi and we drove to the airport. Boarding the flight I handed Adaline our IPad to watch the movie Frozen she absolutely loved the movie. In fact she loved all Disney princess movies. It was cute watching her sing along to the movie and act out some of the scenes.

I hadn't left Adaline's side since the note and neither has Levi. I was worried but I knew deep down that Levi would be their for us no matter what. That's one of the things I love about him, through the short time we've been together I've never seen him give up at the task at hand. He always made sure the pack was safe and happy. That we are safe and happy.

Our plane landed safely in Arkansas. We rushed home Levi had informed Carter of what had occurred during our stay and he was furious to say the least. Nobody messed with the alpha and got away with it.

Once we got inside Levi had us all enter his office for the meeting. Adaline and I sat on the couch having her play her alphabet game while we discussed to major problems at hand.

Not only had we gotten our threatening letters but we also had a few rogues wondering by our territory recently. They were planning something we just didn't know what.

" No one knew where we were going except for the members staying in the pack house. This is why I only allowed you both in." Levi stared looking straight at Carter and his father. They both nodded understanding the importance of the situation.

We both knew the only ones we could rely on were Carter and Tom. They were family and would never break our trust.

We moved a bed into our room to keep Addy with us we also installed alarms on all the windows and in our bedroom. The only people who knew the passcode included Levi and I. We needed complete and total privacy from our pack. We knew their was a mole we just didn't know who.

We went to bed at eight. Closing all the blinds and Locking the doors and checking all window we finally went to sleep.

1 Week LaterLevi

We hadn't gotten anymore letters although we did get more rouge sightings. They were increasing as a very rapid pace. At first it was just on or two a week now their come every day. Their attempting to intimidate us but their failing miserably.

Our pack is one of the strongest in the country. Not only that but we also had multiple alliances.

I had the girls go through practice drills in case anyone infiltrated our borders they were to go into the safe room. The outside was plated with pure silver. I had it specially mad after the letter. Only

Ellie could open it. Inside it was stalled with food and water along with two beds and a restroom.

I had woken up to Ellie pushing me awake the windows alarm was going off. All of a sudden our packs alarms went off we werc being attacked.

"This isn't a drill Ella take Adaline to safe room now!" Ella ran with Addy in her arms. Cody broke through and I was now sniffing the air for the rogue but what greeted me was devastatingly worse than a rogue it was rogues plural. I could smell over a hundred of them. I fought killing them one by one until I saw someone who made my eyes see red out traitor...

Ella

I ran as fast as I could and made it in record time the safe room was hidden behind an cabinet within a desk it was only small enough for children luckily I am as small as a fifth grader opening up the door within the cabinet I grabbed Addy carful to not have her skin touch the door once we were inside I closed the heavy door. The room was practically a vault.

Our ventilation came through two floor vents too small for someone to crawl through and even if they could they were plated with pure silver also.

As we huddled on the bed waiting for Levi to come through the mind link I felt a stab of pain come through my chest. Levi was hurt. I could feel it. I desperately wanted to rush to him help him through the battle. But I couldn't I knew that if I went I'd die and I would leave Addy with Levi or as an orphan. I couldn't leave her no matter how much my heart was fighting me I had my mind win. I felt another stab of pain this one had me holding my hands up to my chest gasping for air as the pain felt excruciating.

" Are you okay. Levi don't give up. I love you! We love you!" I linked through our bond.

"Ella. Love. I'm okay just a little wounded the battle is nearly over. I love you." He responded quickly.

After those words I didn't hear back from him for the next three hours I sat with my arms wrapped around our child hoping and praying for the best. As the pain in my chest continued to grow I knew he was alive I could feel him through our bond what had me worried was how long it was taking him.

Levi

It was him. How could he betray me like this we grew up together sure we weren't as close as Carter and I are but I considered him my fried for crying out loud Ethan was my delta.

"You did this. This is what you want death and for what being the beta? Face it even if you were able to defeat me you couldn't also defeat Carter." I knew I was getting to him, and th fact was I want lying. Carter is one of the strongest wolfs in our pack and I can even say that he's better than me at fighting. Though I wouldn't say to his face he already has a big enough ego.

" You thought you could defeat us?" I question.

" I know you can beat me in a fight but you know what you can't beat?" He sneered and his face turned into a smirk

" A silver bullet."

I had been shot in the chest. The pain was unbearable. Ella has come through our link. "Ella. Love. I'm okay just a little wounded the battle is nearly over. I love you."

" Carter I've been attacked kill Ethan he has a gun be care.." I had drained all my energy and with that I passed out.

CHAPTER TWENTY

Time for School

Hey you guys so His Only Mate has made it to over 900 readers!!!! Thank you for all the support and love

Ella POV

It's been a month since the battle. Ethan was killed after he had shot Levi. Carter had found him andas he was ordered he killed Ethan within seconds.

Levi hasn't woken up for a month now he lays in our bed with wires and tubes connected to him. The doctors claimed his coma is his body's way of healing itself but the sad fact is he's completely healed just hasn't woken up.

The first time I saw him it broke my heart. He looked so helpless, his face was pale and his wounds were bandaged. I haven't let Adaline visit him. Levi wouldn't want her to see him so broken. I feel so bad by not allowing her to see him but I'm scared about the questions it may bring.

Carter and I have been doing all the paperwork for the pack. Jane
has informed the pack on Levi's health the fact that he hasn't woken
up has scared us all. Werewolf's heal faster than others. The doctors
said he should be in a coma for a week not a month and yet here we
are.

After two weeks of him being in the hospital I had him moved to
our bedroom. Theirs a nurse who comes every three hours to check
on his vitals.

Every night I read to him the books I've found in his office. He had a
little library full of the books he loved some where classics and others
were more modern. I had chosen Fahrenheit 451. After reading four
chapters I set the book down and turned to look at the man I loved
his brown hair was disheveled and greasy from his lack of showering
and his facial hair was growing in. Although in my eyes he's still as
gorgeous as the day I laid eyes on him.

I padded my way to the restroom grabbing a towel and took a
shower. I had decided to finally go back to school tomorrow . I
finished washing my hair and shaving. When I was completely rinsed
of I hopped out and wrapped a towel around my body and my hair.

Looking in the mirror I noticed how skinny I had become. After
moving in with Levi I had started to eat everyday and I gained the
weight I needed I looked great my hips finally filled out and I looked
more like a women. Sadly I hadn't eaten the first week Levi was in the
hospital and the second week wasn't much better. Jane has gotten me
to eat more these past two weeks but the worry and stress has ruined
my appetite.

I walked into our closet and grabbed some pajama shorts and one of Levi's T-shirts. While I was walking towards the bed I put my hair up in a big messy bun. Levi was still asleep I laid down in the extra bed we had brought in for Adaline and wrapped the blankets around me welcoming a dreamless sleep.

I woke up to the nurse three hours later. She left and I once again passed out. I woke up to our alarm. I stood up walking over to our alarm clock to turn up off. Levi was still asleep. I leaned down and kissed his forehead.

"Well Levi it's time for school." I said not expecting an answer as I walked away a hand held onto my arm. I turned around slowly to see Levi looking at me with curiosity lurking in his beautiful green eyes.

"Nurse!" I screamed.

The plump old nurse rushed in and to out all the wires and tubes checking his vitals. I grabbed a cup of water and lifted his head to allow him to take a sip. Once her finished I slowly laid him back down.

"W-what happened?" He said with a raspy voice.

" You've been in a coma for the past month. I'm so glad you're awake. I've missed you so much." I cried. Leaning down and kissing him on the lips. Levi deepened the kiss once we pulled away we were both breathing heavily.

Levi tried to stand up and nearly fell down I grabbed onto him helping him up. We walked into the bathroom.

"I want to take a shower" he mumbled I knew he wanted to be alone but in the state he was in he couldn't take one without falling down.

I put the lid to the toilet seat down having him sit on it as stripped my clothes off. Levi's eyes had gotten wide.

"Okay let's take a shower." I said he slowly got up to his feet with my help as I helped him undress. We walked into the large shower I had Levi sit on the shower bench as I washed his hair and his arms and legs. Although I'm other scenarios this may seem sexual it wasn't it was just a job the had to be done. Helping him stand his body was washed off by the spray of the shower head. Turning the water off I helped him sit back on the bench. I wrapped a towel around myself and placed another towel on our bed. Walking back in with Levi I set him down on the towel while handing him another one. As he dried off I picked out an outfit for both of us I settled on some black basketball shorts and a black T-shirt for Levi also grabbing him some boxers. I chose a sundress and grabbed myself some underwear as well I walked into the main bedroom and handed him his clothes. Levi was already getting his strength back werewolf healing.

I got dressed as well and once we were done I held his hand as we walked down the stairs and into the kitchen. Jane and Tom saw Levi first and rushed over to him hugging him and asking him if he was okay if he was still hurt wich he told them he was fine and just needed to get his strength back. Addy screamed as she ran to him. I picked her up and Levi kissed her on the head. Screw school. Everyone was happy as we spent the rest of the day with Levi watching movies.

CHAPTER TWENTY-ONE

Root Beer Float

Hey guys. So my day has been pretty hectic but I still wanna finish my book!!! My school has gone completely online which is crazy!!! So please enjoy .

Ella POV

Levi healed immediately and tonight we are going on another date but this time Jane and Tom are babysitting. I'm so excited to spend some personal time with Levi. Everything we've been through has been extremely chaotic but I'm glad to put it all behind us and have a wonderful day with the man I love.

I've learned many things about Levi Adam Williams over these past months. Levi is strong on the outside but he is also loving inside. I've learned that he loves to cuddle and late night kisses. He likes fried chicken and the color blue because of my eyes. I know he has a little freckle on the back of his left shoulder that's shaped like a star. And I positively know he truly loves me.

As I continued to daydream about our future and all the wonderful things we will do together I was snapped back to reality.

"Ella dear, what are you wearing tonight?" Jane squeaked. She was excited about the date even though she wasn't going.

"I'm not sure ye..." I was cut of by Janes squealing as she ran into the closet throwing clothes around the room. It looked like a tornado had hit my closet by the time she was done.

My bed was covered in different outfits to choose from. As I looked at all my options my eyes landed on a beautiful dress white and yellow lace dress. It was gorgeous and I instantly grabbed it running to the bathroom to put it on.

It fit me perfectly the bottom flared out just below my knees. Looking in the mirror I spun around enjoying the turn of the skirt.

Walking into the room Jane looked stunned. I knew I looked different this dress made me look more mature, more like a Luna. I had already been introduced as their Luna but now I looked and acted the part. I was their for the pack no matter what.

Jane curled my hair as I applied rosy red lip gloss, sparkly eye shadow and Better Than Sex Mascara. Once I was satisfied with the outcome I grabbed a beaded purse and put on some white heels.

Walking out of our room I walked into Addys to find her sitting on the floor in one of her princess dresses playing with her Barbie dolls. When she heard my heels she looked up her beautiful blue eyes laced with excitement as she ran to me wrapping her little arms around me.

"Mom were are you and daddy going?" She asked sweetly.

"We're going on a date. Why don't you and grandma make us a vanilla cake with extra frosting?" I smile sweetly. She loves cake but not as much as me.

She nodded immediately and ran off to Jane most likely to ask her to make a cake. I walked into Levi's office to see him leaning over a stack of paperwork. He was dressed in a nice suit waiting on me. Right when I walked in he looked up at me with a big smile spreading across his handsome face.

" You ready to go? And where are we going?" I questioned. I was too excited

"Now why would I spoil the surprise? Don't worry you'll love it." He replied.

Levi

Tonight is the night. Tonight I'm going to propose to my love. I bought her a beautiful ring it's a bit big but at least every human will see she's taken.

I planned to take Ellie to an old soda shop where my grandpa met my grandmother. It's a small vintage shop that I want to share with her.

Ellie held my hand as we walked to the car. Thanking me when I opened her door.

"Why can't you tell me where we're going" she whined I could tell that Ellie was becoming impatient.

"Babe where almost their you'll love it trust me." And with that we arrived.

It was located in town in a small old strip mall. The store known as LuLu's has old fashioned candy, along with salt water taffy and homemade pop tarts.

My grandmother fell in love with the small shop and as their wedding present he bought her the shop. It became a hobby of hers she would bake homemade pop tarts and make people shakes. When my grandparents passed away they left the restaurant to me.

I helped Ellie out of the car and as she saw the shop her eyes grew wide and her jaw dropped. When her shock finally settled she ran inside looking at every little thing from the pink chairs to every kind of chocolate and candy in the shop. She also looked at the menu making faces as she looked at every option until she found the one she wanted.

"I'll have a root beer float and some fresh apple fritters please." She said smiling at the lady at the counter. It only took a minute for the lady to make her order and afterward I ordered a chocolate milkshake. Once we got our drinks and fritters we walked over to sit at a table in the back of the shop.

"This place is amazing! Oh if I didn't work at Charlie's I'd work here. Look at all the pastry's they make!" She gasped

"Would you like to work here?" I questioned if she wanted to work her she will work her and if she doesn't want to work than she doesn't have to.

"Yes! Totally! But if you hadn't noticed they don't have a sign up for help needed." She said sadly.

"Well you're hired."I stated smiling at her.

"You own the shop?" She whispered. Leaning across the table.

"Yes. I do. Actually the family does." I smiled at her as her smile grew wide and then she squealed in excitement telling me about how much she wants to learn to bake the recipes work at the bar.

"Ellie?"

"Yes" she said sweetly looking up from her float.

"Do you love me?" I asked starting to get nervous.

"Of course I love you." I blew out an anxious breath as she responded.

I stood up from my seat and kneeled on one knee.

" then will you do me the honor and be my wife. Ellie I knew the second I saw you that you were perfect for me and once the bond happened I knew it was the moon goddess telling me that you were mine and I yours." Once I finished speaking I pulled out the ring as Ellie gasped with tears In her beautiful eyes.

She nodded her head and finally said the word I was waiting for.

"Yes" she gasped "Of course I'll marry you." She screamed as she jumped into my arms kissing my face as she hugged me as if her life depended on it. The other patrons in the shop cheered.

Grabbing her shaking hand I slid on the ring. And we returned to our kissing fit.

Ella

Everyone was asleep when we arrived home Levi and I walked into our bedroom. Once I got in I was pushed against the wall as Levi's arms trapped me in.

Leaning down his lips settled on mine at first our kiss was slow but soon it was rapid and full of lust and passion I moved my arms around Levi's neck rubbing my fingers in his hair he moaned and grabbed my hips pulling me to him their was no space keeping us apart.

I pulled away turning my back to him Levi unzipped my dress letting it fall to the floor leaving me in just my underwear and shear bra. Grabbing me he pulled me close kissing my lips and moving down my neck and onto our mark and I instantly felt tingles electrify my body. Moaning in response Levi growled leaning away to take his shirt off and lifting me up to throw me on our bed before me hovering above me.

Looking deep into my eyes. He asked me for my permission to give him the most valuable thing a woman has to offer her heart and love.

"Are you sure?" He whispered.

I nodded and we spent the rest of the night making love for the first time.

CHAPTER TWENTY-TWO

The Wedding

Ella POV

I woke up on top of Levi's warm body his arms were wrapped around me preventing me from leaving him. I tried to move from his grasp to feel a throbbing pain from in between my legs making me flush at the thought of what we did last night. Levi opened his eyes to look at me. He was really sexy in the morning his bed head was cute but the lazy grin he gave me really put me over the edge. He leaned to kissed me but I turned my head so he kissed my cheek. Looking back at him I could tell he wasn't happy by my action.

Raising my hand over my mouth I whispered " morning breath."

Levi rolled his eyes at me taking one of his hands of my waist the grab my hand in his as he leaned in once again to give me a soft kiss on the lips. Leaning away he smiled at me.

"How do you feel like this morning?" He asked with concern written all over his face.

" I'm just a little sore." I replied untangling myself out of his grasp to go to the restroom. He let out a sigh as I walked away into the bathroom butt naked. After I finished doing my business I brushed my teeth and went into the closet to pick out an outfit for today. I have no doubt that Jane already knows I'm engaged. As I'm going through my clothes I fell Levi's arms wrapped around my waist as he bends down to put his head on the top of my head.

Today was Monday I'm a little upset that we dont get to stay home today but I've missed enough school this year and I need to go. I settled on wearing a blue button up shirt with a cute little plaid skirt that matched with my white vans and a star charmed necklace. As I collected what I'd be wearing I went into the bathroom to take a shower.

As I was walking Levi was right on my trail. I turned the shower on and waited for the water to heat up once it was warm I hopped in. I was in the middle of putting shampoo in my hair as Levi walked in to join me. He washed my hair and put conditioner in it. As I washed my body with body wash. Levi did the same.

I decided to leave my hair down after brushing through it. I did my eyeliner and put on some blush and lip gloss. Looking in the mirror I saw a hickey on my neck. I can't believe I just noticed it. I can't believe he gave me a damn hickey. I started looking through all the drawers and cabinets looking for concealer but came up empty out of all the products I had I didn't have concealer or foundation.

I ran out of the bathroom and out of the bedroom no doubt scaring Levi. I ran all the way to Jane and Toms bedroom, knocking on the door Jane came over to open the door she was already awake and dressed for the day. "Do you, um, have any concealer?" I asked as my face became as red as a tomato. Her eyes landed on my neck and she began to laugh and nodded welcoming me in as we walked into her bathroom. She handed me her concealer thankfully we shared a very similar skin tone so it didn't seem as though I was wearing makeup walking back into our room I went into the bathroom and began to apply it to my neck. Levi walked in as I was doing so and gave out a grunt.

"What's wrong?" I asked him.

"Why are you hinding that?" He asked hurt laced in his reply.

" Because girls are mean and rumors go around fast." I stated. It's true and sad if a girl walks into school with a hickey people think of her as easy or a slut whether or not she is in a relationship.

Levi nodded and came up to me and gave me a hug. I know he doesn't want me hiding any sign that says I'm his. Leaning back I held up my left hand which held my engagement ring. "I'm not hiding this" I stated smiling up at him. This made him smile and kiss me again. Leaving the conversation their I walked over to Addy's room in order to wake her up.

I spent the morning preparing breakfast for us and then I had to go to school. Levi was waiting for me in front of our class. I saw two girls give me dirty looks. That's something I've noticed more. Girls really do like my mate but the problem is he loves me and is all mine.

At lunch we saw Avery and Carter waiting for us at the tree. Nobody noticed the ring for awhile but once they did the cat was out of the bag. Everyone knew we were engaged.

Many people said we wouldn't last that we were dumb because we are only kids. But when I truly thought about were we ever really kids? Levi has been trained and pushed into the role of alpha at a very young age. I never had the chance to be a kid because I was taking care of myself. Although we come from different backgrounds we both were never offered the ideals of being a child and neither would our future heir.

It's sad to think about but also true. I had two wonderful years of being a child and that left with Anna. I want my children to have what I couldn't. The love that Levi gives me is what makes me forget about the past and think about our future.

We spent the last month of the school year planning for our wedding. Avery's my bridesmaid/maid of honor, Carter is the best man, Adaline is going to be my precious flower girl, and our ring bearer is our new Delta Tyler.

The girls (Avery, Addy, and Jane) and I went dress shopping and also got ourselves pampered at a spa. I had my nails done in a light pink. When we went to the dress shop we were surrounded by beautiful wedding dresses. Looking around I tried on a few that the girls picked out but my eyes landed on one in the back of the store it was white and off the shoulder in a somewhat vintage fashion. It was simple it had a band which was covered in jewels across the mid waist.

I knew this was the dress I'd be walking down the isle to meet my husband. When Jane saw me she cried tears of joy and so did I. We blubbered and paid for the dress. I was so excited our wedding was next week. It's common for werewolves to get married soon after they meet their mate but because I'm human Levi and I took it slower well somewhat slower.

~~*~*~*~*~*~*~*~*~*~*~*~*~

Today's the day in getting married Levi and I slept in different rooms last night which was awe full. All I wanted to do was snuggle into my man.

Jane woke me up and had me shower and dry myself off. Once I was done I was put in a rob as stylist's entered and started prepping me for the wedding my hat was done in a cool curly braid thingy down my back which had flowers and pins placed in. My makeup was flawless it was natural and not too thick but the thin eyeliner brought out my blue eyes and the rosy lipstick matched my complexion.

We chose to have our wedding by the forest. It was beautiful the area which now had lights streaming around and a small little path leading me to my future husband.

Levi

She looked outstanding. I can't believe this angel is mine.She is best woman to ever walk into my life. Having her as my mate, my wife, and the future mother to my children is better than anything imaginable.

We said our vows and in the blink of an eye she was all mine we had it written and bound by our undying love.

My wife is my life, along with our family no matter what happens I know we will get through it together.

CHAPTER TWENTY-THREE

Epilogue

Five Year's Later

Ella POV

Not long after our wedding I had gotten pregnant with Ryan. He's the sweetest boy ever he has my dark curly hair with a sea green eyes. He's built like his daddy and active like him too. Less than a year after Ryan I got pregnant with Mathew he has blonde hair and blue eyes he looks strikingly similar to Levi's fathers.

After our three I said I was done. But god has a funny way of bringing in surprises. I ended up pregnant again a year later with the twins Jackson and Jacob. They are both identical little versions of Levi except Jackson's more gentle. That was it I thought but of course our condom broke and now we're pregnant with number six.

I was so happy when I discovered I was having another girl. I knew Addy wanted a sister when I first got pregnant but now at nine years old I think she's done with babies. So now we're having Isabella.

Levi got what he wanted a huge ass family and I got a bunch of Angels with some stretch marks.

It's funny to think about being twenty three and having six kids. And yet here I am.

I love my huge crazy family.

Levi

"Push baby you got this" I said as Ella gave me the death glare.

"You Fucking did this to me six goddamn times your getting sniped or I'm leaving" she screamed as she pushed again. I'd admit that when she said she didn't want anymore I was a bit bummed but seeing as we have six little monsters running around our house I can understand.

"One more push" the doctor said and out came our daughter. They took her and had her cleaned. She looked just like her mom. Finally one of our babies is identical to my wife. She already had some hair on the top of her head it was blond so maybe she wasn't identical but she had the same little nose people get surgery for and the same heart shape face. She was going to be a heartbreaker.

"Okay" I said. It hurt my manhood to admit it but having children is taking a toll on my beautiful wife and if she doesn't want anymore that's okay.

"Babe I'm sorry for saying that I'm just going on birth control." She replied sweetly.

I laughed and looked down at our little princess. Boy was I going to wrapped around her little finger.

The End